For Alex, it has always been Gina. And maybe it always would be, whether she could see it or not.

In that case, he could only cross his fingers and hope that she would catch her next plane as soon as possible, because he didn't think he could bear to watch her settle down and find her happily-ever-after in Peach Leaf without him.

And now she was staring at him and he hadn't said a word in a very long time.

"Small towns, huh?" she said, her voice teasing but warm, eyes studying him as she waited for a response.

"Can't go anywhere without running into someone you know," he added.

Gina released a little puff of air. "Unfortunately, that's true." A hint of darkness clouded her features.

A beat passed as her words sunk in.

"Oh my goodness!" She reached out and the tips of her fingers brushed his arm, sending a tingle over his nerves. "I didn't mean it like that. I don't mind running into you, really. That came out wrong."

Her complexion turned an even rosier shade, and he had to look down at the toes of his sneakers so he wouldn't be tempted to touch her again.

Dear Reader,

If this is your first time in Peach Leaf, Texas, please let me extend the warmest welcome! And if you're returning to this charming little town, I'm so pleased to see you once again!

It's been a while since my last story, and I would love to say that there is a happy reason for my extended hiatus. But the last several years have taught me that sometimes it's more helpful to open up about challenges than it is to paint a cheerful picture when circumstances are anything but. I've come to believe that when we share our struggles, there is a chance our experience might help someone else who is going through something similar.

Between my last book and now, I went through a period in which my mental health suffered deeply. Thanks to a wonderfully empathetic doctor, my incredible husband and a scrappy rescue dog named Maggie, I made it through. It wasn't pretty or easy, but here I am. I still have tough days, of course, but with treatment and support, I've been able to find bright spots among the darkness.

And, just like Gina does in this story, I've had to pause and ask myself—what comes next along this journey?

I hope you'll join Gina as she figures out her next adventure and gains her own supportive hero in the process. And if you ever struggle with mental health as I have, I hope you'll find a way to reach out for help. You may discover that you're stronger than you think, and that this life—while not without challenges—still has much beauty to offer.

Happy reading!

Amy

Starting Over
at Trevino Ranch

AMY WOODS

HARLEQUIN

SPECIAL
EDITION

HARLEQUIN®
SPECIAL EDITION™

Recycling programs
for this product may
not exist in your area.

ISBN-13: 978-1-335-72466-3

Starting Over at Trevino Ranch

Copyright © 2023 by Amy Woods

For questions and comments about the quality of this book, please contact us at CustomerService@Harlequin.com.

Harlequin Enterprises ULC
22 Adelaide St. West, 41st Floor
Toronto, Ontario M5H 4E3, Canada
www.Harlequin.com

Printed in U.S.A.

Amy Woods loves lazy, book-filled afternoons, walks with her senior rescue dog and watching movies with a husband she adores. She lives in central Texas, where sunshine and tacos are never in short supply. Visit her on Facebook at AmyWoodsAuthor or follow her on Instagram @amywoodsauthor.

Books by Amy Woods

Harlequin Special Edition

Peach Leaf, Texas

Puppy Love for the Veterinarian
An Officer and Her Gentleman
His Pregnant Texas Sweetheart
Finding His Lone Star Love
His Texas Forever Family

Visit the Author Profile page
at Harlequin.com for more titles.

This one is for Carly Silver, who pulled me from the slush pile long ago and supported me during the early years of my writing career. Many happy wishes on your next adventure!

Chapter One

"Dad would for sure disown me if he saw what I'm doing right now," Gina Heron muttered under her breath as she scrolled down the page on her laptop screen. She must have started and abandoned the application for unemployment benefits at least ten times since breakfast, and she still couldn't seem to manage looking at it for more than a few minutes at a time without that familiar queasiness kicking up again.

"Well," Gina's sister, Sophie, responded from her spot facing a nearby bookshelf, where she'd been organizing new travel titles for the last half hour. "Dad's not here, is he? So, I wouldn't worry too much about him judging you." Her tone was gentle.

"I know, I know," Gina said, rubbing her temples as she released a sigh. "But he always chided us to 'never take a handout' and in my head I've got a track on repeat of him saying, 'when things get hard, you've got to pull yourself up by your bootstraps.'" She crossed her arms for emphasis, just like Dad would have done.

Sophie put down the book she'd been holding and moved behind Gina, wrapping her arms around her sister's shoulders. "To that I would say, it's pretty damn hard to pull them up when you don't have any straps to speak of…not to mention boots."

Gina giggled softly, thankful for her older sibling's steadfast sense of humor.

"Besides," Sophie continued, squeezing Gina's shoulders before heading back to her work, "it's not a handout. It's *your* tax money, there for a rainy day when you need it." She picked up the next book from a box near her feet, briefly studying the cover. "And goodness knows you've had plenty of storms recently." Sophie paused. "I just wish I could afford to hire you myself. It would be so nice to have you working here with me—" she turned and gave Gina an apologetic look "— for actual pay, I mean."

Gina closed the laptop with a little more force than was probably necessary, earning a sideways

glance from a customer browsing the shelf closest to her.

That was enough for one day. The application
wasn't going anywhere, so she could continue staring at it tomorrow, hoping for some magic to happen so she wouldn't actually have to go through
with completing it. Her sister was right, of course,
and in her heart Gina knew she had no reason to
feel ashamed for needing a little help until she got
back on her feet, but a piece of her didn't want to
admit defeat. Until she actually hit Submit, Gina
could keep pretending that her life hadn't suddenly
erupted into a total mess.

Standing up to stretch, she glanced out the front
window of Sophie's small-town Texas bookshop,
Peach Leaf Pages. Late afternoon sun washed over
the sidewalk, and passersby, clad in T-shirts and
shorts for the warm spring day, carried to-go cups
of tea and coffee and brown paper bags of goodies
from the café next door as they browsed the deco-
rated storefronts along Main Street. A vanilla latte
sounded perfect, but Gina cleared all thoughts of
delicious hypothetical treats from her mind as she
headed to Sophie's closet-sized office in the back
to use her sister's one-cup coffee maker instead,
visions of dwindling bank account balances danc-
ing in her head.

Today marked one month since Gina's latest

teaching contract had ended, and she had yet to land another offer.

Since graduating with her master's over a decade ago, she had moved seamlessly from one teaching position to the next. Specializing in English as a Second Language instruction for professional adults, her skill set had always been in demand overseas, and she had never struggled to find work. She'd spent many happy years bouncing across Asia, enjoying the incredible people, food and cultures she encountered each time she took a new contract, all the while promising herself she'd find a more permanent position and settle down one day in the distant future.

She had never imagined that the timing wouldn't be her choice, that she'd be forced to stop moving against her will, before she was ready. But it seemed as though all of her colleagues with the placement agency had already found new positions or had chosen favorite locations to build lives. Meanwhile, Gina was stuck in her small hometown, treading water while her savings, and the little extra money she brought in from her tiny, word-of-mouth upholstery repair business, continued to decrease at an alarming rate.

Gina shook her head to clear away regret over a reality that no longer existed. She could keep her head in the clouds all day, but where would that get her? There was only one way to look at it now: at thirty-six, she would have to start all over again, and, having already achieved and lost her dream job, she had no idea how to do such a thing, or where to even begin. As thankful as she was that Sophie had been eager and happy to share her tiny space with her younger sister, Gina yearned desperately to regain her self-sufficiency.

"Oh, my gosh! I'm so sorry to hear that."

Gina turned abruptly at the worry in her sister's voice. A woman in her midsixties with cropped salt-and-pepper hair, sporting a stiff-looking back brace, grimaced in obvious pain as she spoke with Sophie, urgent tension in her voice.

"It's okay," the woman said, glancing woefully toward the children's section. "I'll heal in time, but I don't think I can sit through the reading today. I hate to leave you in the lurch like this, but I've got to get home and lie down. I'm due for meds soon and, until things get better, I'm having to take them like clockwork."

"Of course, Noreen," Sophie said, her words soothing as she followed the woman to the front of the store. "You should have just called, you poor thing. I would never have asked you to come in if I'd known you were in this condition. Dan must be worried sick."

Noreen waved a hand in dismissal. "Oh, he

knows I'm a tough old bird. My back gives out every once in a while, so we know the ropes by now. The trouble is, I never know what's going to set the darn thing off. It'll be good as new before you know it, and I'll be back reading to the little ones."

"They'll miss you big time," Sophie said, holding the door open for the injured woman, who walked stiffly through, waving toward a sedan parked on the street just outside. The man in the vehicle—presumably her husband—got out of the driver's side and moved quickly to help his wife.

"There's Dan now," Noreen said. "Take care. My apologies again," she added with warm sincerity, hands clasped in front of her midsection. "I hope you can find somebody to take over."

"Oh, don't worry about us," Sophie called, smiling as Dan rushed over to take Noreen's hand. "You just concentrate on getting well."

As the couple got settled in their car and drove off, Sophie waved goodbye and closed the front door, setting off a pleasant chime of bells. She leaned against the solid oak and closed her eyes, pulling in a deep breath as if to center herself.

"They seem sweet," Gina mused, watching the car go.

"Yeah," Sophie agreed, opening her eyes as she

stood upright again. "They've been inseparable since they were kids."

A little shard of pain sliced through Gina. She had known a love like that once, long ago. Or at least she'd thought she had.

It became clear that Sophie's attempt to relieve her tension hadn't worked. She glanced in the distance over Gina's shoulder and bit her lip, worry filling her light brown eyes. Gina followed her gaze to the children's corner, a sweet alcove tucked in the space between two tall, blue-painted shelves full of picture and chapter books, adorned with cozy pillows, colorful carpet squares and sparkling strings of fairy lights.

"What's the matter?" Gina asked.

"Noreen was our children's reading hour volunteer." Sophie swallowed hard and looked down at her watch.

"So, you'll find another volunteer," Gina suggested. "Surely you've got a backup." But, as they'd been talking, Gina noticed that a few kids had started gathering on the carpets, their parents taking seats in a row of chairs set up just behind.

Sophie's head was moving slowly back and forth, and her teeth were making such a dent in her bottom lip that Gina worried she'd soon draw blood.

"So, I'm guessing…you don't have anyone else who can do it?"

"That's right," Sophie said, planting a hand against her forehead. "It's one of the million things on my to-do list that I keep thinking someday I'll have time for. Until you came to help out, it was about as long as Main Street, and it's getting shorter, but…"

"But you had a regular volunteer so that item wasn't at the top," Gina said, filling in with a growing sense of apprehension. She had an idea where this was going.

Sophie dove right in. "Come on, Gina, please?" She pulled up prayer hands in front of her pleading face.

"Um," Gina said, closing her own eyes so she wouldn't fall victim to her sister's huge, pleading, abandoned baby bunny ones, "I don't think I'm the right person for the job. You know I don't have much experience around kids." She swallowed anxiously.

"*Please*," Sophie said, the strain in her voice tugging hard at Gina's heartstrings. "You're a teacher, though. That's close enough, right?"

Gina stopped and dug in her heels, facing her sister as she steeled herself to be as firm as possible. "I teach business ESL *to adults*. Not exactly the same thing." She pulled her shoulders back, eyes darting about the shop as she desperately avoided meeting her sister's. "Now, if you'll excuse me, I believe I've got another round of job applications to fill out."

Sophie's expression softened. "Look. I know this is a little out of your wheelhouse. I wouldn't ask, but the kids are already here, and they'll be so disappointed if I cancel story hour."

Gina scanned the group of small humans as she considered her sister's request.

"Gina?" Sophie said quietly, reaching out to grasp her sister's arm.

"What?"

"It's just…you look nervous," Sophie said, a hint of a giggle in her voice. "They're just children," she soothed. "They won't bite."

"You cannot guarantee that," Gina argued.

Sophie grimaced. "Well, you're right about that. But I can say they've never bitten Noreen, and that's something, right?"

Yeah, she looks sweet and all, but my sister can be pretty conniving, Gina thought.

Sophie assumed a serious expression and continued, "We're running out of time here, so are you going to help me or not? And, before you answer, remember whose couch you slept on last night."

Gina's mouth opened wide and her eyes narrowed. "Oh, that's low, Soph," she chided, clicking her tongue, even as she silently prepared to give in to the inevitable. She knew she couldn't leave her sister like this, not when there was a crowd gathered already and parents were starting to check the time impatiently.

Gina knew Sophie had put her heart, soul and years of saved-up dollars into her bookstore, and she'd worked her butt off to get it off the ground, even as nearly everyone around her said that brick-and-mortar book sales were a thing of the past. As she watched Sophie wring her hands, Gina knew what she had to do, and dammit she would do it.

"Fine," she said, her insides melting as Sophie's face lit up with gratitude, her pale cheeks regaining the color they'd lost. "But you owe me."

Sophie started to speak, probably to remind Gina again about the couch and the free roof over her head, but Gina stopped her.

"You owe me." She rolled her shoulders a few times and cracked her knuckles, preparing for the lions' den. "Two margaritas as soon as we close up. No negotiations. Take the deal or I'll walk." Gina fixed a steely gaze on her sister.

Sophie's lips trembled as though she might laugh. The nerve.

"I mean… I won't walk far, but, you know… back to the office to work on the books or something," Gina said, afraid she'd been a tad too harsh.

Only a tad, though.

"Deal," Sophie said, holding out her hand.

Gina shook it, very reluctantly, glaring additional death rays at her only sibling.

"Wonderful. Thank you so much!" Sophie bounced up and down. "By the way, the book is on the big chair in front of the kids." She snorted. "You'll be reading, *Tomorrow I'll be Brave*, by Jessica Hische."

A favorite of her sister's, Gina knew the book well, and the pertinence of its title, as well as the book's message that it's okay to be scared when trying new things, did not escape her. With a deep breath, she crossed her fingers and hoped she could live up to it.

No matter how hard he tried, Alex Trevino seemed doomed to fail when it came to getting his niece and nephew to their various activities on time.

He'd always taken pride in being early to events and appointments. As his *abuelo* taught him growing up: "on time equals late, and early equals on time"—advice he took seriously and continued to live by, and that had served him well for all of his thirty-seven years. Advice that seemed impossible to live up to when it came to kids.

His heart softened as he glanced in the rearview

mirror at ten-year-old Eddie and six-year-old Carmen, wondering how it could possibly have taken so long to get them into his pickup. There must be some sort of time vortex when it came to children; it took twice as long to get them to accomplish anything as you thought it would, and even if you started getting ready early, the extra time somehow didn't add up the way it should, as if each minute flew by in only thirty seconds.

He must have made himself chuckle because Eddie asked, "What's so funny, Uncle Alex?"

Seeing no other vehicles on the sleepy ranch road, Alex turned quickly to smile at his nephew. The little boy had inherited the Trevino family's dark hair and eyes, and his mother's endearing dimples. "Oh, nothing much, bud." Alex turned back to face the road. "Are you guys excited about story hour?" he asked hopefully. He would do anything in his power to cheer them up these days.

"Meh," Eddie responded. "Story hour is for little kids, but I'll go because Carmen needs me to look out for her."

At this declaration, a lump formed in Alex's throat. It was a tender sentiment from a protective big brother, even if it was only half true. He knew for a fact that Eddie, an avid reader since age five, absolutely loved story hour, and really, any story he could hear, see, or get his hands on. That kid was going to become some kind of writer when he grew up. Alex would bet his family's ranch on it. On top of that, Eddie was just an all-around good kid, who had put his whole heart into looking after his little sister since their parents—Alex's older brother and sister-in-law—had lost their lives in a plane crash the year before.

Becoming Eddie and Carmen's guardian had been a whirlwind of lawyers, documents and packing up their things to move in with him, the tasks providing an escape from his own grief. Having gone from bachelor to caregiver overnight, Alex hadn't had a chance to deal with his own pain, and, while he'd been thankful for the distraction at the time, some days he wondered if he should spend some time finally processing everything that had happened, maybe even get some counseling…if he could ever find a spare moment.

Alex turned onto Main Street and located a parking spot near Peach Leaf Pages, then got out to help the kids from the back seat, taking a small hand in each of his. As the bell on the shop door chimed, announcing their arrival, Alex quickly noted that the children's area was already full, and the other kids were fully engrossed in the story.

So much for sneaking in without disruption.

He knew he shouldn't be surprised. Noreen Connelly, retired sixth-grade teacher—his, actually—was a stickler for punctuality, even when she wasn't on the clock, which meant this marked their third week of making a far more conspicuous entrance than he would have liked.

Oh well, Alex thought, guiding Eddie and Carmen toward the reading circle, hoping there was still a spot left for each of them. Not much could be done about it now. As much as he'd like to, he couldn't turn back time any more than Cher could.

"Okay, guys," he said softly. "Let's be as quiet as possible so we don't interrupt the story."

He gently squeezed each child's hand and led the way.

"But how will we know what's going on?" Eddie asked quietly, mild frustration in his voice. "The new lady's already started reading."

"Yeah!" agreed Carmen, much, *much* less quietly than her brother, prompting an aggravated "Shhh!" from someone in the group.

Probably Kenneth, resident taskmaster. Aged five. Relentless enforcer of story hour etiquette, with a disapproving scowl that burned all the way to your toes.

Alex briefly closed his eyes, drawing in a breath. Okay, so maybe they needed to spend a little more time working on inside voices, at least before his niece started kindergarten the following year. He was definitely in support of a woman with a strong voice who knew how to use it…just…maybe not during story time.

"Carmen, sweetheart, let's try to whisper," Alex said, demonstrating. "And, Eddie, it's okay. We're only a few minutes behind. I'm sure you'll be able to catch up on the plot in no time."

He got his two settled with the other kids and moved farther back to find a seat among the other parents and guardians, who, thankfully, adjusted knees and purses to let him pass, probably having been in his shoes before. Maybe not as often as he had, but still.

Smiling gratefully, Alex finally slid into a chair of his own, just as something Eddie had said before caught his attention.

What *new lady*?

Noreen had been the only story hour volunteer every time Alex had brought Eddie and Carmen for the past several months, and as far as he knew, she had no desire to give up her position. The kids adored Mrs. Connelly. She did all the voices in the books, was so animated that Alex was certain she could have had an Oscar-worthy acting career if the teaching hadn't worked out, and she even used props and wore homemade, highly accurate character costumes. Likely there weren't many people lining up to take Noreen's place in the high energy, paycheckless endeavor. Plus kids that age were a tough crowd. Alex was pretty sure they could smell fear, and probably parental inadequacy too, which he had plenty of.

Taking *guardianship* of Eddie and Carmen had been an easy choice; he loved his niece and nephew and it was simply the right thing to do. He'd been in their lives from infancy, spending time with them at family events, never missing a single birthday or milestone, and babysitting when his brother and sister-in-law went on anniversary trips. Taking *care* of Eddie and Carmen, on the other hand… nothing had ever been more challenging.

Having wanted his own kids someday, Alex had never been naive enough to think that parenting would be an easy job, but he hadn't even remotely grasped how utterly *big* it was. Not just the day-to-day tasks involved in keeping two small humans alive, dressed and fed, and getting them to the places they needed to go, but the deeper stuff. The questions he couldn't answer. The philosophies he hadn't yet considered about how best to develop these two into good people, good citizens, good stewards of their gifts and resources who cared for their community and planet and…it was a *lot*.

He wasn't prepared, and he was slowly beginning to understand that maybe nobody was. Maybe nobody *could* be, not fully anyway.

In the meantime, he did the only thing he knew,

which was to give his best moment by moment and hope it added up to something that would serve those kids well, because they'd sure as hell been through enough already.

A cheerful voice pulled his attention back to the present. Wait…there was something familiar about that voice. It set off a mosaic of memories—little pieces that didn't quite add up to anything solid, but made him feel a thousand hazy things at once. Spring rainstorms and a majestic show of lightning from the vantage of a barn loft; a summer day on a dock down at the reservoir, a beach towel for a picnic blanket; the high school football stadium, just before kickoff, a small hand in his and a soft voice encouraging him, easing the jitters that sometimes got so bad his stomach would hurt just before he had to go out on the field…

That voice. He'd recognize it anywhere.

And yet.

Alex looked up in disbelief. It couldn't be her. She was gone—had been gone for years now. Not enough to make him forget, unfortunately, but enough to ease the hurt to a point that he'd been able to build a life that didn't include her.

It was then he noticed that the reading had stopped—in fact, all noise around him had ceased—and the entire row of parents, the kids on the carpet and the customers milling around the bookshelves…

all had their eyes on him. Briefly, it crossed his mind that this level of unwanted attention should make him pretty damn uncomfortable, except that he couldn't really process any of it.

Not when Gina Heron, the love of his life, the same girl he hadn't seen in nearly two decades and had in fact never expected to see again, was staring straight at him.

"Um, excuse me, miss," interjected Kenneth the future hall monitor, pointer finger raised. "The story?"

Unable to take his eyes off her, Alex watched as Gina cleared her throat and forced her concentration back onto the slim chapter book that sat closed in front of her. Sliding from her lap as she startled, it took a dive and landed with a quiet *smack* at her feet, splitting the continued silence. She glanced down, not seeming to register what had happened until a little girl picked up the book, handed it back, patted her knee reassuringly and returned to a spot on the carpet.

Gina shook her head. "Thank you," she said to the little girl, eyes wide.

"Uh, okay," Gina said, thumbing through the pages until she found where she'd left off. "Let's continue."

Meeting Alex's gaze one more time before quickly pulling her eyes away, she picked up where she'd left off, her voice shaking a little from time to time until she regained her footing.

Alex closed his eyes and pinched his thigh, hard, through his worn jeans, but when he opened them back up, she was still there. Daring to look to his left and right, he was relieved to discover that he no longer captured the attention of everyone in the room. The parents around him had resumed reading email on their cell phones and the shoppers were once again browsing, no longer curious about the sudden silence in the children's corner, and all was as it should be.

Except that Gina Heron, the woman he'd promised his heart to at age eight, the woman who'd turned down his marriage proposal after they'd planned a life together—the woman he'd tried with all his might and yet failed to stop loving—was apparently back in town. Add to this that not a single soul, not even Gina's sister, Sophie, who knew damn well that he and the kids showed up weekly for story hour, had thought to pass along this epic news.

To make matters worse, seeing her didn't just bring back all the bad stuff, all the heartache she'd caused. Looking at her now—that halo of untamable, curly gold hair, the almond-shaped light brown eyes that nothing slipped past, and those sweet soft curves he'd lost himself in so many times—it was easy to pretend that not a moment had been lost between them.

Too easy.

The room began to spin a little, and Alex's breath came in shallow spurts.

He couldn't just leave. It wouldn't be fair to the kids, who needed routine and consistency and who looked forward to story hour. It would be selfish to disrupt their time just because he couldn't manage to get it together. All because of a woman he should have gotten over ages ago.

Chapter Two

I am going to kill you, Sophie Alice Heron, and scatter your remains in Marty Montalvo's chicken yard, Gina thought, seething, even as she wondered whether or not the lovably eccentric older guy still named his favorite fowl after country western singers. Her personal favorites had been Waylon Hennings, Dwight Yolkum and Tanya Clucker.

Focusing on the task at hand, she plastered on a smile for the kids. They didn't need to know that the person reading them a cute story harbored homicidal thoughts toward her older sister.

Her traitorous older sister.

How could Sophie not have told her that Alex might bring his kids to reading hour? How could

Sophie not have told her that *Alex had kids*? He had to, because he was sitting back there in the parent chairs, staring down at the floor to avoid making eye contact with her.

For the love of all things holy, her sister owed her that much.

Alex had been the love of her life, and he had broken her heart. Even though she'd had to do it, leaving town, leaving him, after graduation had torn her to pieces, so many in fact that she'd almost failed at putting them back together. This information wasn't something her sister could have just forgotten, and as soon as these kids stopped staring at her, and the chapter was over…oh, she and Sophie would have words.

Just don't look at him and it will be easier, Gina told herself. She only had to get through this, and she could walk straight past the front desk and right up the narrow staircase at the back that led to her sister's apartment above the shop. It wasn't that hard.

Thanking the stars when she saw that the next page was only half-filled with words, the bottom portion a blank void of white space, Gina managed to finish the last bit of the story without having a panic attack or making a run for the door.

"And that's it for this week," she said, her voice so loud and unnaturally pleasant she was pretty sure she scared a few of the kids. "I'm sure…*some-one* will be here next week to pick up where we've left off."

As the little ones began to disperse and reunite with their parents, her eyes darted around the bookstore to locate her sister, but her vision was cut off when a girl Gina guessed to be about six years old came up and stood before her, shifting from leg to leg.

Crap, Gina thought. She'd done her sisterly duty and filled in for the absentee story hour reader. Surely she didn't have to entertain follow-up questions. Kids always seemed to cut right to the chase, to ask the hardest questions—ones she, even as an adult, never quite knew how to answer.

"Miss?" the girl said, bouncing on her heels.

Gina closed her eyes to calm her racing heart, then opened them slowly.

"Yes?" she asked, meeting the little girl's eyes. They were umber in color and warm, set deep in a heart-shaped, tawny-beige face. As much as she didn't want to be, Gina surprised herself by responding to the kid's widening grin with one of her own. The girl gingerly placed a little hand on Gina's knee.

"I really liked how you read the story," she said, before turning on her heel and running straight for Alex.

Of course.

Gina's smile dissolved.

It was ridiculous not to have recognized those familiar features, even in another person's face. The hairs on the back of her neck stood as realization settled in. *Of course* Alex would have moved on, met someone else and started a life without her—a life that obviously included children.

What had she expected? That he would, what… wait for her? Really. She'd never given him any indication that she would come back and, in fact, hardheaded and stubborn at eighteen, she'd promised quite the opposite. It was a move that brought her sorrow nearly every day since. She'd made the decision to walk away from a lifetime with Alex; at the time it had seemed the right choice, at least to her young heart.

Growing up in Peach Leaf, with a distant, reluctant father had been difficult and isolating. Small towns weren't always friendships and potlucks and festivals. Sometimes it was loneliness, being surrounded by people who knew what was going on at home, who saw their dirty clothes and unkempt hair and knew how hard things were for her and Sophie, but who hadn't lifted a finger to help because it might have gotten messy.

Staying and building a life among the prying, judgmental eyes of her neighbors had never appealed to Gina, especially not when there was a great big world out there she wanted to explore. A life of travel and new experiences had called to her, and she hadn't been able—hadn't wanted—to resist.

Yes, there were moments here and there when she questioned her decision, but that's what life was: a series of choices. When you made one, there wasn't always the opportunity to turn back, and the years were too short to waste wondering what might have been. So, you moved on, and you did the best you could.

And yet here she was in the same room with him again, a place she never thought she'd be, and he was walking in her direction.

"Hey, Gina," Alex said softly, his expression guarded.

The simplest greeting, and yet it had the power to unravel her. The years of wondering whether she'd made the right move, of thinking about him every day whether she wanted to or not, of not being strong enough to throw out that old football jersey that followed her from one apartment to another no matter how far back she shoved it in a drawer…

Looking straight into his eyes, unable to find the right words to say, her heart would know him anywhere.

It was Alex. The Alex she'd loved so long ago.

Time had done little to change his features. He had the same deep brown eyes and tawny skin as the tiny girl who clung to his leg—though the sun had burnished his a shade darker—and the muscles under his shirt and faded jeans were hardened from ranch work.

He must have done what he'd promised, she thought, and taken over his family's decades-old business. It had been a point of contention between them all those years before, but she could see now that it appeared to suit him.

"Hi," she responded, her voice surprisingly steady considering the surge of complicated and confusing emotions swirling around in her brain.

Gina wished she'd never come back to this town, with its inescapable memories and history that had a grip on her. She knew she didn't want to spend her whole life in Peach Leaf. That's why she'd left all those years ago—to escape. At the same time, it was home, and everybody knew you could only run so far from it. And the biggest part of her history was standing right in front of her, pulling her back into a world she'd been so sure she wanted out of. So sure...

"So, you're the new storyteller?" Alex asked, studying her with an intensity she'd always found unsettling. He had known her so well for so long that the smallest change in her expression could tell him what she was thinking without a word spoken. It was both overwhelmingly comforting to be known that deeply, and disquieting because he was the one person she could never truly hide from.

"Ah, no. Definitely not," Gina answered. "I don't have much experience with kids."

"Odd way to spend an afternoon then, don't you think?" Alex mused. His expression had softened and a corner of his lips ticked upward.

He was teasing her, she understood suddenly, inviting her to lighten the moment with him, and she was thankful for the gesture.

"Let's just say it wasn't exactly in my calendar," she said, grinning, her nerves loosening a little as she talked. "Sophie needed me to fill in for Mrs...."

"Connelly," Alex finished for her.

"Right," Gina said. "Noreen injured her back, so here I am."

"Sophie owes you one, doesn't she?" he asked, his lips splitting into a grin that reminded her why she'd been drawn to him in the first place.

Oh jeez. If she had any sense, she would walk straight out that door. Anything but stand there and watch those dimples start to get under her skin again. If she had any sense...

"You bet she does," Gina answered. And it was the last thing she could think of to say because, really, where would this end? What was the point of having a conversation at all, when she had no intention of digging up the past?

He was watching her again, little grooves at the corners of his intelligent brown eyes telling her he had at least some idea of her unspoken thoughts.

"Well," she said, "I've got to put this book away and get back to work."

His eyebrows perked up. "Oh, you're working for Sophie now?" Alex asked. "I know she's needed help for a while. This place gets so busy on the weekends. It's nice that you came back to town to do that for her," he said warmly, a hint of deeper interest underneath the polite, safe statement.

In lieu of explaining, Gina simply offered a resigned smile and pointed to the shelf behind him. "It's nice to see you again, Alex. If you'll excuse me, I've got to shelve this and—"

"Get back to work." He nodded. "I know."

He moved closer to her, so close that she could smell the cinnamon mints he'd always favored. The scent, once a balm to her nerves, now prompted a wave of sadness that hit her like a storm wall.

Tight-lipped, she waved the book in front of him and ducked her head to silently pass by.

"Here," he said, his voice soothing as he followed. "Let me help."

"I don't—"

"Please." Gina heard so much more than a simple word when he said it.

Avoiding his gaze, she held out the volume and Alex gripped it, his fingers grazing hers, their touch no less charged now than it had always been.

Pulling it gently out of her hand, Alex walked toward the bookshelves in the children's area, Gina unable to keep from following closely in his wake like a tugboat tailing a ship. He scanned the titles until he found the spot where it belonged, then used his thumb to mark the space.

"Ah," he said. "Here we go."

Reaching up, he almost had the book in place when suddenly, the little boy he'd brought with him appeared at his side and gave a tug on Alex's jeans. Startled, Alex dropped the book, which bounced right off Gina's head before landing on the carpet with a thud.

"Ow!" she cried out.

Gina had only just reached up to rub the newly sore spot when Alex's fingers grazed her hair, his hands gently cupping her face.

"Oh my God, I'm so sorry. Are you okay?" He bent down to stare into her eyes and all she could do was stare back, neither of them realizing for several seconds that any time had passed at all. He was comforting her, caring for her as he would have if they'd never parted ways, and she let him, completely unable to move herself to stop it.

When Alex caught himself and pulled his hands away abruptly, tucking them into his pockets as if they burned, his reaction smarted far more than the bump on her head.

Gathering her wits as she brushed stray curls from her brow, Gina nodded. "Yeah, I'm all right. It's just a little sore."

"I'm so sorry, Gina. I never meant to—"

The sound of giggling erupted behind them, and they looked down to see Alex's kids doing a very poor job controlling their laughter.

Alex frowned and chided softly, "Hey, guys, it's not nice to laugh when someone gets hurt."

But it was too late. The musical sound of the kids' giggling mixed with Alex's very serious expression, plus the need to release some of the morning's tension and the awkwardness of running into her childhood sweetheart, let something loose inside Gina. In a single moment she was laughing as well, and the kids were laughing even harder, and then Alex was laughing, too, and...

"It's really okay," she said when she'd calmed down enough to speak. "I know you didn't mean to hurt me."

"I truly didn't," Alex said. His smile faded and

he looked at her for a long time, making her very self-aware. "And I am sorry."

"We're sorry too," said the little boy who looked like a miniature version of Alex. "We didn't mean to laugh. I hope you're okay." He glanced shyly down at his sneakers.

Gina's throat went dry, and there was a tickle behind her eyes. "Oh…that's okay," she said. "I know it's hard not to laugh when someone gets bonked on the head, and I'm not hurt."

"Aren't you going to kiss it?" the little girl asked suddenly, twirling a finger in her dark hair as her eyes darted between the grown-ups.

"Uh…what?" Alex asked, blinking as the tops of his ears turned pink.

Gina folded her lips together and put a hand over them, trying hard not to smile.

"Kiss the nice lady's head," the girl said, pointing toward Gina's noggin with an exasperated huff, as if she could hardly be bothered explaining the obvious. "When I get hurt, you kiss it and make it better. Aren't you going to kiss her head where you dropped the book? You have to make it better." She raised her palms as if to say, "Duh!"

Gina supposed she could have made things easier for Alex, but it was far more satisfying to watch him squirm. What happened next, though, she couldn't have prepared for.

"She's right, you know," Alex said, his eyes softening as he narrowed the distance between them, causing her breath to hitch. "I did in fact drop a book on you, and who knows, you might even have a knot there soon thanks to me, so the least I can do is…"

Reaching out to gently grasp the tops of her arms, he leaned over and pressed his lips to her crown, holding them there for longer than he should have, but perhaps not as long as she would have liked.

"All better now," Alex whispered, brushing his fingers against her cheek before pulling away slowly, his deep brown eyes meeting hers.

So much passed between them in that single look that Gina couldn't bring herself to speak, despite her mouth opening and closing several times. Alex, of course, noticed this and seemed to take joy in the fact that he still had the ability to undo her, a fact that would have annoyed her if she'd been able to feel anything other than pure shock.

The kids were staring wide-eyed when Gina finally regained control of her body and glanced their way. "I, uh, I guess I'll, uh…"

"It was good to run into you, Gina," Alex said, his eyes darkened with mischief. "We'll see you around."

Alex reached out his hands and the kids took

one each, waving at her as the little family headed back through the store. When they reached the front door, he glanced back once before opening it to leave, his expression too complicated to read.

"Not if I can help it," she whispered to herself as the door closed behind them.

Seeing him this once had shaken the already wobbly ground she'd been teetering on since losing her job. Until a month ago, there had always been a next step, a new job in a new country, another destination to run off to. Gina didn't know if she had the courage to face the past, to unpack her troubled childhood and the people she blamed for looking the other way, to make amends for leaving Sophie—and Alex—for so long without ever stopping in to see if they were okay.

A question nagged at her from somewhere deep inside.

How will I cope if I have to stay still for a while?

"I hear what you're saying," mused Vanessa Green, Alex's best friend and owner of Knot Your Average Crafts, a yarn and crochet shop on Main Street. "It's just that I don't believe you."

Vanessa raised her eyebrows pointedly as she continued sorting through a new shipment of patterns.

The shop was quiet on a Tuesday morning. Alex

had stopped by to say hello after taking the kids to their dentist appointments. He'd assigned the morning's tasks at the ranch to his most trusted hand, but he knew from experience that not being there to participate in the work himself would nag at him for the rest of the day. Then again, so would his best friend if she knew they'd come into town without stopping by.

Alex threw up his hands in defeat. One of the things he loved most about Van was her straightforward honesty, but that didn't mean it was always easy to swallow.

"I mean it," he said, pushing back, still reeling from seeing Gina only a few days before. "Every word. I definitely kissed her."

"On the head," added Carmen absently, utterly enchanted as she stroked the new purple-and-turquoise shawl Vanessa had made for her.

Alex had known the second his friend lovingly bestowed the colorful gift on her that his niece would be wearing it nonstop for at least a month, and he wouldn't be allowed to wash it even though he'd been given very clear instructions on *how to do it the right way*. His standard ranch clothes weren't exactly high maintenance, so when he became a father figure he'd made a mistake here and there in the laundry department, among others, and boy had he gotten an earful.

Vanessa's husband, Darian, had been the ac-
countant for Trevino Ranch for nearly a decade
and the first time Alex had invited the couple and
their two kids over for dinner, Vanessa and Alex
had bonded instantly over their shared love of mystery novels and true crime. The families had been
inseparable ever since, and Alex knew he would be
completely lost without the couple's patient advice
and steadfast support when it came to parenting.

Though Alex's mother insisted on helping as
much as possible, she was getting older and had
already done the work of raising children of her
own. He knew she adored spending time with her
grandchildren, but Alex didn't want to take advan-
tage of her generosity, and he felt that she deserved
to enjoy her golden years as she pleased.

He loved Carmen and Eddie, deeply, and he was
more than happy to be their guardian, but when
he'd imagined having a family of his own, those
dreams had always included a partner, someone to
share the burden of managing his family's ranch,
as well as the challenges that came with raising
small children.

Vanessa stopped unpacking the new stock and
looked straight at him, her mahogany eyes wide,
tight curls bouncing as she tilted her head. "So,
the kids really did see you kiss your long-lost high

school sweetheart?" she asked, pointing a finger between them and him. "On the head, apparently?"

Gina was so much more than a high-school flame, but Alex just rolled his eyes. "Makes me feel so good that you'll take the word of a six-year-old over your best friend."

Van's lips rose in a mischievous grin. "I know I can always trust Carmen to tell it like it is."

"Truer words…" Alex said, sharing Van's smile. Carmen told the truth, loud and proud, no matter where they were, who the audience was, or how embarrassing it might be.

"I guess it was just an in-the-moment reaction," he explained, shrugging as he stuffed nervous hands into his pockets. "I know it doesn't make sense, but after all these years of not seeing her, it felt like…no time had passed." He couldn't help the tickle inside his chest at the thought of the woman he'd loved so much for so long. She'd hardly looked any different, which added to the strange feeling that maybe almost two decades hadn't actually slid by in which they'd built separate lives. If anything, the added years only agreed with her, as if the passage of time had simply polished her best features.

Something flickered across Vanessa's expression, and Alex knew she worried about him. And to be fair, why wouldn't she? While he tried not to dwell on the past too much, and didn't see the point in wishing for a life he'd once dreamed of, he had certainly talked about Gina a few times, and Van knew his heart had never fully healed after the breakup.

It probably seemed troublesome to Van that he had made such a bold move when keeping his distance would've been a smarter choice. If Gina was back in town, regardless of how long she planned to stay, he couldn't expect to avoid her entirely but he sure as hell could've been a little bit smarter, a little more protective of his banged-up heart. Because along with the joy of seeing her again—that frisson of happiness at the sight of a face he held dear—there was an ache as well, of old wounds resurfaced.

"Listen," Vanessa said, her voice warm with friendship but nonetheless firm, "I'm not going to tell you what's best for you—you're a grown man and that's your job to figure out—but I am going to tell you to be careful, because I do *want* what's best for you and I don't want to see you hurt again." She shoved the box aside and put her palms down on the counter in front of her. "I wasn't here when you guys were together, but I know that what happened between you left scars you've worked hard to heal. Don't forget the weight of that work."

Alex nodded with gratitude, swallowing hard.

Her words were so insightful that he had to take a deep breath to regroup.

"Enough about my past," he said, changing the subject as he went to pull Carmen's perpetually sticky hands from a boxed set of crochet hooks and redirected her to join her brother. Eddie was sorting glass beads by color and texture, a task Van always left open for him when they came in, knowing how much he enjoyed the soothing activity. "I want to hear what's new at Chez Green, and if you've read anything good recently."

Van's eyes lit up, and Alex was grateful for her willingness to switch tracks with him.

"Nothing much at home. Darian's still trying to rope me into trying his raw food recipes and I'm still not having it, and yes, I have read something good! There's a new one out about a group of community college students who went missing from Peach Leaf in the seventies. Of course, I won't tell you how the case went down." She winked and wiped her hands on her slacks, disappearing into her office at the back for a second before rejoining him with a hardcover, which she handed over. "I didn't want to wait for the library to order it, so I went ahead and bought it for myself. You can borrow it when I'm done, which won't be long because it's nearly impossible to put down and I'm sneaking a few pages any chance I can."

He read the inside cover and handed it back. "Looks intriguing," he said. "I need something to distract me anyway…from things."

"This'll do it. Made me never want to go for a walk in the woods again, though, I have to say," Van added with a little shiver.

"Perfect," Alex answered, and the two friends shared a smile just before the shop door chimed announcing a customer, or, just as likely in Peach Leaf, a friend.

Alex and Van looked up at the same time.

A talented businesswoman and welcoming person in general, Van called out a friendly hello and, tossing a quick glance back at Alex, headed toward her new customer to see if she could offer any help. He, on the other hand, stood completely still, as if one of the kids had hot-glued his shoes to the floor.

Gina.

Chapter Three

She hadn't yet noticed him, so he figured he still had a few seconds to decide what to do: buck up and greet her like a decent person, or take the easy way out and slink off like a coward.

He wasn't proud to admit which one appealed to him more.

Not to mention Van would never forgive him if he was rude to a customer in her store, known for its warmth and nurturing community.

He rubbed his brow and took a deep breath. He supposed if he had to talk to Gina twice in one week, he might as well get it over with.

Her cheeks deepened to a darker shade of pink as he approached, and he guessed she was reliving what happened at the bookstore.

He sure was.

The light coconut scent of her shampoo and the softness as his lips had brushed against her hair, the way his blood heated as he'd drawn near… same as it did now. She was intoxicating—or was it just plain toxic? Her presence made it hard to tell, the memories rushing back again as he'd begun to suspect they would anytime they were in the same room together.

He had always believed she was his person, the one he was meant to spend his life with. As a teen, when the other guys on the football team had been talking about the various girls they'd dated and how thrilling it was to be single and available, Alex always counted his lucky stars that for him, the search was over. He'd found his love early on and hadn't wanted anyone else.

The memory of her had made it hard for him to date anyone else. Their early, easy love, the way they fit together comfortably and joyfully, made dating feel tense and awkward, like squeezing his foot into the wrong size boot. He knew it wasn't fair to the women he'd gone out with, but he was always searching for another Gina, knowing full well there was only one.

For Alex, it had always been Gina. And maybe it always would be, whether she could see it or not.

In that case, he could only cross his fingers and hope that she would catch her next plane to far-away lands as soon as possible, because he didn't think he could bear to watch her settle down and find her happily-ever-after in Peach Leaf. Without him.

And now she was staring at him and he hadn't said a word in a very long time.

"Small towns, huh?" she said, her voice teasing but warm, eyes studying him as she waited for a response.

"Can't go anywhere without running into some-one you know," he added.

Gina released a little puff of air. "Unfortunately, that's true." A hint of darkness clouded her features.

A beat passed as her words sunk in.

"Oh my goodness!" She reached out and the tips of her fingers brushed his arm, sending a tin-gle over his nerves. "I didn't mean it like that. I don't mind running into you, really. That came out wrong."

Her complexion turned an even rosier shade, and he had to look down at the toes of his sneak-ers so he wouldn't be tempted to touch her again.

"It's okay. I knew what you meant."

"It's just… I can't even grab a burger without someone squealing and saying how long it's been, as if I don't know when I last visited," Gina explained, her eyes showing a spark of humor. "I'm surprised no one's gone so far as to actually pinch my cheeks and tell me how grown-up I've gotten."

"Well," Alex responded tentatively, "I won't pinch your cheeks—" at this, Gina giggled, the sound sweet and sparkling like champagne "—but I'm afraid small-town politeness does require that I ask how you're getting on these days."

As soon as the words were out, Alex wished he hadn't said anything because the light left her eyes, along with that pretty smile he'd always been willing to do just about anything to earn.

Everything in him told him he shouldn't have offered more than a simple greeting. Even Vanessa, wearing a stern look, was trying to catch his eye, as if to warn him of a *no trespassing* sign up ahead. But something pulled him on, made him want to keep Gina in the room despite the glaring fact he didn't have a hold on her anymore. She hadn't been *his* for a long time, she wasn't his now, and forging this path would probably lead him straight down an empty road ending in a thorny patch.

With an audible sigh, Gina glanced around the room, seconds passing in silence as she took in the cubbies full of yarn arranged to form a rainbow that filled the entire back wall of the shop, and the cozy corner filled with plush chairs Vanessa allowed crafting clubs to use as they pleased.

His gaze followed hers as she noticed the kids. Carmen had joined her brother and was helping him with the beads, and Gina gave a soft smile as she watched them together. Carmen waved wildly when she spotted her new favorite story hour reader, but Alex was surprised to see Eddie raise a palm as well, though his expression remained serious and he quickly went back to sorting beads. Sometimes his nephew showed little interest in people outside their family circle, a challenge Alex suspected they would have to work through together in the near future.

"I could tell you that everything is fine," Gina started, her tone heavy with some unseen burden, "but you would see right through the lie."

Her eyes met his and she tucked a loose, shining wave of flaxen hair behind her ear. She wore a brightly patterned knee-length skirt and teal top with Birkenstock sandals. Alex had always loved her unpretentious but cool, comfort-first style, and her penchant for choosing only the brightest colors. Her outer appearance matched her inner self; her knack for finding joy in the most ordinary occurrences—a tiny frog jumping across a sidewalk, the smell of flour from a freshly opened bag, her light-hearted eagerness to kick off her shoes and sink her toes into the lush green grass on a spring day.

But only a few people closest to her, Alex included, knew those aspects of her personality were hard-won. Gina and her sister had a rough time of it growing up, but with strength, resilience, and each other's support, they had always managed to keep their heads above water.

Seeing her now, with an obvious weight on her shoulders, had Alex's hackles raised against whatever might be threatening her happiness. The problem was, he couldn't let her know how much he wanted to guard her from life's hardships, or she would run away again, and the more time he spent in her vicinity, the more he wanted to fight to keep that from happening. It didn't seem to make a difference that she was no longer his to protect.

Unable to say anything close to what he was thinking, Alex just nodded, hoping against all reason that she would open up to him like old times, as if they'd never been apart. Even though she hadn't let him love her the way he'd wanted to—a choice he'd done his best to respect—he was still allowed to care about her. Maybe there was something he could do to help and maybe, if he trod carefully, she might tell him what that was.

"The truth is, after my last teaching gig ended, the placement company I worked for shut down, and I haven't been able to land another position. I really don't know what to do next," she said on a puff of air, as if she'd been holding it back for a long time. "I haven't told anyone except Sophie."

It went without saying that Sophie would keep the information to herself. The sisters had that kind of bond.

"I'm so sorry to hear that," Alex said.

Gina nodded with a sad smile. "That's why I came back to town." Her chin jutted forward. "Just until I can find a new job and get back on my feet," she added in a stronger tone.

"Of course," he answered. "It happens to a lot of people at some point or another."

Now that chin tilted to the side as she studied him. "Not you," she said. "Your family's ranch has always been around, even when others have folded."

Her eyes softened, and Alex heard respect and understanding in her voice rather than the resentment that had been there each time the subject came up when they were younger. She had always wanted to run, to get away from Peach Leaf, a town that, for her, held scars and tough memories alongside the good ones. Their hometown wasn't as warm and safe for Gina as it had been for him, and Alex had always known deep down that she would leave.

He had promised to join her, at least for college, before deciding whether he would take over the ranch or make a different choice, but his father's unexpected heart attack had left Alex, barely eighteen, without a choice, so he'd said goodbye to Gina and stayed behind. He didn't blame her for leaving without him, but a part of him had wished she'd stayed to hold his hand during those tough years. And now that he'd adopted his niece and nephew, and even more challenging times lay ahead, he found himself wishing the same thing again.

"Maybe you were right to stay," she added.

Alex's response caught in his throat. It was something he'd always wanted to hear, and had imagined her saying many times…but not under these circumstances. Somehow, being right didn't seem as important anymore.

"Do you have a place to stay in the meantime… I mean until you get back on your feet?" As soon as he said it, he realized what a dumb question it was. Of course she'd be staying with Sophie, and if Alex knew Sophie, it would have been made clear that the invitation was open as long as her sister needed it.

Gina surprised him by releasing a little laugh

as a hand flew up and she lightly tugged at a yellow earring in the shape of a stegosaurus. "Yeah, I do. I'm staying with Sophie, but…"

He arched an eyebrow.

"Never mind," she said, waving away the thought.

"No, it's okay." He reached out a hand, nearly touching her, but quickly forced himself to pull it back. "You can tell me."

The truth was, as much as he didn't want to admit it, he'd like to sit with her for hours and catch up on everything that had gone on in her life since she left town. What had it been like to take that big leap and move overseas right after college? What cities had she visited? What was her favorite place she'd lived so far? And…had she found what she'd been searching for…that nebulous sense of peace and happiness he hadn't been able to provide?

No way in hell was he going to say that out loud.

"Really?" she asked, scrunching up her nose. "After everything that happened and all the time that's passed without even an email between us, you really don't mind hearing about the minor drama of my life?" Her eyes danced with amusement.

"It's you," he said, shrugging, his voice barely audible even to his own ears. "You can tell me anything."

But she'd heard. He thought he saw a glimmer of moisture shine in her eyes for a second, but it was gone in a heartbeat.

Alex gestured in the direction of Van's chairs and Gina headed that way, him following. Van, who, after greeting Gina, had resumed taking inventory of her new stock, caught his eye. Her expression was inquisitive but not judgmental, and he loved his best friend all the more for it.

Alex glanced toward the kids to make sure they were still safely occupied before taking a seat across from Gina. He grinned as she sank into the oversize chair and leaned back, closing her eyes.

"God, this chair is everything," she said, kicking out her legs. "Maybe I can just rent one of these and live here forever."

"No way." Alex laughed. "If Vanessa finds out you're in need of a place to stay, she'll have you living in her guest bedroom by the end of the afternoon, and you'll have your own monogrammed towels a week later."

"Hey!" Vanessa called out. "I'm not that bad." She came up behind and swatted his shoulder. "I'm just fond of having guests."

"It's one of the many things I like about you," he said.

He caught Gina's curious glance out of the corner of his eye, and it occurred to him that she might mistake the nature of his and Van's relationship.

"Vanessa's my best friend," he added quickly. "She and her husband have been friends of mine for a long time."

Gina's shoulders seemed to relax a little. Not that he was concerned…

"I'm Gina, an old…acquaintance of Alex's. It's so nice to meet you," she said, reaching out to shake Van's hand.

"Oh, the pleasure's all mine," Van said, a sparkle in her eye that set Alex on edge. "I've heard so much about you."

He braced himself even as Gina gave her a shy smile.

"So, I hear you need a place to stay," Van said.

Gina waved her hand dismissively. "Oh, no, I'm okay. I've been staying with my sister."

"With Sophie?" Van asked skeptically. "In that tiny little apartment above her shop?"

Gina winced. "Yeah."

"Oh, you can't possibly be comfortable up there. It's barely big enough for one person. She showed me her space when she opened the store. It's adorable, don't get me wrong, and it's perfect for Sophie, but it wasn't built for guests."

Gina issued a little laugh. "You're not wrong.

She was even talking about moving out, renovating and opening up the space to expand the store."

"Yeah," Van said, tapping a finger to her chin. "I think she mentioned wanting to put a journal and art supply section up there."

"Yes," Gina agreed. "That is, until I moved in."

Van made a sympathetic noise. "Oh, I'm sure she's happy to have you. She was so excited when she found out you were coming back to town."

"I'm not back, exactly," Gina said quickly to correct her. "Just visiting until…for a while."

She looked embarrassed at her almost-admission, and Alex's heart ached for her.

"Well, if you're here for a while, then you need a bigger place. And I just happen to know someone who has just such a place."

When he looked up, Van was staring at him with wide eyes and a determined expression, as if he was supposed to be picking up some telepathic message or something.

"Who, me?" he asked, pointing at his chest.

"Yeah, you." She rolled her eyes when he didn't immediately figure out what she meant.

Then, suddenly, it dawned on him what she might be getting at. He frowned.

"You mean the old shack down by the river?"

Van nodded emphatically and poor Gina looked…hopeful.

He shook his head and scoffed. "That place has sat unused for years. My parents boarded it up after the last of the ranch hands moved into a house in town years ago. It's probably a mess."

"It is not *an old shack*. It's a super cute cottage. Sheesh! Good thing this guy doesn't write real estate listings, right?" She winked at Gina and then turned to Alex. "And if it needs some work, then get someone to fix it up," Van added with a lot more enthusiasm than Alex felt. "Oh—" she clapped her hands "—it'll be a perfect job for Jesse!"

His younger cousin, a few years out of an apprenticeship, was in the early stages of setting up as a contractor. Jesse was skilled and hardworking. A job like that would keep him busy for a few days and give him an influx of much-needed income.

Alex swallowed. He couldn't argue with cold, hard facts and very reasonable ideas. "You're right. It would."

He looked up at Gina and caught the obvious hesitation in her eyes.

"It's okay," she said, false nonchalance in her voice. "I'm fine staying with Sophie. I don't want you going to any trouble, and I won't be here for very long anyway."

"Nonsense," Van said, shooting a stern look at Alex. "It's the perfect place for you. Quiet, cute, with a gorgeous view of the river, and you'll have your own bedroom and bath. That's got to be a heck of a lot better than sharing with your sister." She nodded for emphasis. "And the ranch has surprisingly strong Wi-Fi."

Sophie and Gina had shared tighter spaces than that when they were kids, Alex knew, and he could tell Gina was having the same thought as he watched her turn the idea over in her mind.

It had probably been tough having her foundation shaken after years of steady teaching contracts. It must have brought back memories of childhood, of never knowing whether her father—a decent handyman when he could manage to sober up—would make the rent that month or not, hopping from one cheap apartment to the next.

Suddenly, he wanted nothing more than for Gina to move into that old cabin, and he would call Jesse immediately and have it fixed up so nice she wouldn't be able to turn it down.

"Vanessa's right," he told her. "It's a good cabin, and I can make it comfortable in no time." He paused. "Rent free, of course…for you."

What the hell am I doing?

Both women looked at him, Van with smug triumph that her inarguably excellent plan had been accepted, and Gina with surprise and what looked like a little bit of nausea thrown in.

Alex backtracked quickly. "I mean, you would be doing my cousin a favor. He needs the work and this would be the perfect fixer-upper job for him. Plus it's not being used anyway, so you might as well..."

Gina's eyes flew to her lap. "It's a really nice offer," she said, before pushing out a slow breath. "And I'm grateful for the kindness."

She glanced between him and Van, brows knit and eyes full of turmoil.

With a pang, Alex realized that he was hanging on her every word, waiting to see if he would get the chance to have her back in his life, if only for a little while...

"But there's no way I could accept it."

Alex and Van were still sitting there speechless when Gina excused herself and escaped out the front door, as if flames were biting at her heels.

The two friends looked at each other in surprise, and Alex realized he should be relieved at dodging a bullet. There was no way having Gina so close by was a good idea. The focus needed to be on staying away from her, on keeping as much distance between them as possible. Falling in love with her again—if he'd ever really fallen *out* in the first place—would only end in getting his heart broken a second time around. He'd barely survived the first and wasn't sure he could pick himself back up again.

And now there were kids to think about. They needed all he had to offer; there wasn't room for anyone else.

So only one question remained. Why did he only feel…disappointment?

Chapter Four

Gina stared into the ice cream freezer, knowing full well that whatever flavor she chose wouldn't matter when the main objective was numbing her feelings into oblivion with sugar.

Sighing, she closed the foggy door, empty-handed. There was no shame in choosing to eat one's feelings on occasion, but doing so had become a crutch lately, and she knew from experience that the longer she kept up that pattern, the more difficult it would be to break. Unfortunately, ice cream wasn't a good substitute for putting on her big-girl panties and facing her problems.

"I've always been partial to pistachio," said a familiar voice behind her.

Turning, she found herself face-to-face with Alex. Again.

Speaking of patterns.

"I know it's not the most popular flavor, but that just means more for me."

He regarded her with a smile, his brown eyes warm.

Moving aside so that he could reach into the freezer behind her, she gripped the handle of her basket tightly, redirecting her nervous energy into the cool metal.

"Is this a new welcome committee tactic?" she asked, shivering as she suddenly registered the frosty air she'd released by holding the door open for so long. "Following someone around town until they give in and agree to attend whatever social event you've got in mind?"

Gina regretted her words immediately, realizing that her sarcastic comment might come across as rude. Thankfully, Alex picked up on her attempt to lighten the tension with humor.

"No hidden potluck agenda here," he said, holding his hands up in mock surrender before placing them back on the handle of his grocery cart. "Just picking up a few things before I get the kids back from Vanessa and head home."

He paused, the heavy silence lingering between

them. She wondered if he felt the same way she did, that there were so many things to say it became impossible to pick just one. Finally, he spoke. "You seemed pretty freaked out back there...about the cabin, I mean."

She swallowed. "I'm sorry I left so suddenly. That wasn't fair. Vanessa was lovely and it's actually very tempting, but I—"

"No need to explain. I was thrown for a loop, too." He lifted his palms. "If it helps, the offer was sincere. Van surprised me when she brought it up, but once I considered the idea, I realized it really would be nice to have someone occupying that cabin again, for lots of reasons. Keeping critters away, discouraging bored teens who wander onto the ranch..." He searched her eyes. "But listen, why don't we start small? Maybe with dinner? You can check out the land, take a look at the space—if you promise not to judge it too harshly before it's been fixed up, that is—and see if you might be interested." He watched her, an endearingly childlike eagerness in his expression. "No pressure coming from me, though. Truly."

Gina leaned against the freezer door, using the cool glass to temper the anxiety of seeing Alex more times in one day than she had in the last eighteen years. Would he really do this for her, after all this time, and with nearly two decades of unspoken hurt between them? Or maybe it didn't matter that it was for her. Maybe he would have made the same offer to any acquaintance who needed an affordable space.

Alex was that kind of man—generous and selfless, as evidenced by the fact that he'd taken in his niece and nephew to become a full-time caregiver, as Sophie had explained to her—and if he was still the same guy she'd known, she knew he would have done so without hesitation or complaint. These thoughts warmed her, but she tried to focus instead on the practicalities and the fact that a better situation for her was unlikely to come along. Rental properties were not abundant in small towns like Peach Leaf, and Gina really wanted to give Sophie her space and privacy back. She needed a cheap place to stay, and he'd offered one. It didn't have to be more complicated than that.

"Okay," she said finally. "Dinner sounds like a good idea."

He issued a little sigh, which sounded a bit like relief.

"Do you want me to bring anything?"

"Just yourself," he answered, with a smile that resonated through her. "I'll cook, and we'll keep it low key. Any new food allergies or preferences I should know about?"

"No, but it's thoughtful of you to ask," she said, her lips turning up as she remembered how capable he was in the kitchen.

He'd cooked for her when they were in high school, and she'd been unable to rely on steady meals at home. Before that, when they were much younger, it was chocolate chip cookies and carrot sticks after school, or sometimes even a home-cooked dinner with his family, when Gina would ride the bus to Alex's house and wait for her father to pick her up. Or, more often than not, for Alex's mom to drive her back to their neglected apartment building on the edge of town, her father oblivious to the whereabouts of his younger daughter. And many weekends, she had simply spent the night in Alex's twin bed with the superhero sheets, while he chivalrously took to the floor in a sleeping bag.

"How does tomorrow night sound?" he asked, the earnestness in his expression reaching deep into her, making it impossible to back out.

"Tomorrow night sounds great," she answered, surprised by the truth in her own words.

"Good," Alex said, reaching out to gently touch her forearm, the sensation of his fingertips lingering on her skin. "I'll look forward to it."

* * *

"You will not believe what I've just agreed to," Gina said as Sophie entered the galley kitchen in her little home above the bookstore.

Kicking off her shoes, Sophie hung her keys and purse on a hook by the door and went to the sink to wash her hands. Gina pulled the last of the microwave meals from her canvas tote and stowed it in the freezer before finding a spot in the fridge for her Chardonnay. Whatever resolve she'd had in the ice cream aisle had worn out by the time she'd reached the wine section.

"Wild guess—Alex offered you a cabin on his ranch, rent free, and you turned him down," Sophie said, deadpan.

Gina slammed the fridge door much harder than was necessary and turned to her sister, eyes wide in disbelief.

"How on earth did you hear about that so fast?"

Sophie stopped drying her hands and cut Gina a look. "Oh, little sis, you truly have shed your small-town ways and become part of the bigger world. Shall I impart my quaint wisdom upon you?"

Gina rolled her eyes and picked up the empty grocery bag. "Okay, point taken. It was Van, wasn't it? From the craft shop?"

Sophie crossed her arms and stared at Gina. "Well, now I take back my commentary. You know the source of the gossip and you haven't even *met* her!" She raised her palms. "Of course, it's a few steps removed, since I actually heard it from Kelly at the bank, who heard it from Audrey at the market, but still—" hands on hips, she scanned Gina up and down "—I'm impressed."

Gina felt her cheeks warm. "Actually, I have met Vanessa. Just a couple hours ago. Hence my surprise at the speed of your news." She hung the tote next to Sophie's purse. "Has the grapevine updated with the times? Is it a fiber-optic internet vine these days?"

They stared at each other for a second and then burst into laughter.

"I've got some other stuff to catch you up on, too," Gina said when the giggling had calmed down.

"Then," Sophie replied, reaching for the refrigerator door, "we'd better go ahead and open that wine."

Gina wasn't surprised that, after spilling all the details about what had happened at the bookstore and then at the grocery store about the cabin rental,

Sophie had begun a full-force mission to convince her to take Alex's offer.

If she didn't know better, Gina might even think her sister was trying to get rid of her, but Sophie was a romantic, happiest when the people she loved were living in harmony, and she had always been fond of Alex. Encouraging Gina to move onto his property was probably just Sophie's wishful thinking that they might rekindle their old flame. Gina had done her best to quell that notion, but standing there now, at Alex's front door, she couldn't help but wonder if her own motives were entirely practical.

Seeing Alex again had been simultaneously more difficult and more natural than she'd expected. The feeling that they'd hardly spent any time apart was countered by the ache that spread in her when she added up all the years she'd missed, thinking of the ups and downs they'd endured separately.

She was meant to have been by his side all this time. Maybe a better person, a stronger person, would have stayed.

Thankfully, she didn't have much time to dwell on her thoughts, as the heavy wooden door opened a few seconds later and she looked down to see Carmen bouncing up and down with giddy energy.

"Hi, Miss Gina!" the girl shouted at the top of her little lungs. She spun around, twirling the hem of her purple skirt and waving a plastic wand with a star at the tip. "Do you like my new dress? It's my favorite color and Uncle Alex says it's too fancy to play outside, but I'm not really outside if I'm just by the door." Her eyes sparkled as she waited to hear her guest's opinion.

"It's beautiful," Gina said, earning a joyful grin.

"Thank you for answering the doorbell, sweetheart," Alex said, entering the foyer behind his niece. "But can you step back just a smidge so our guest can get inside?" he added, catching Gina's eye over the little girl's head.

"Oh, yeah. Sorry! Come in, Miss Gina," Carmen said, stepping aside and waving her arms in her very best welcoming gesture.

Gina was thankful for Carmen's bubbly enthusiasm, which provided some distraction from Alex's appearance. Wearing an apron over a blue-and-gray flannel shirt tucked into dark jeans, his feet clad in gray socks, he was the picture of country comfort and *home*, and Gina was taken by an overwhelming urge to fold herself into his arms. Time had done nothing to suppress her memory of being with him, and she could practically close her eyes and remember the feel of his embrace, the way she'd once fit so perfectly against his form.

But she was an adult and—despite the presence of Carmen's magic wand—this wasn't a fairy tale, and she had long since given up the right to touch him.

So she took a deep breath and stepped into the ranch house that had always been his home, doing her best to appear relaxed.

"Welcome," Alex said as Carmen skipped around them, grinning from ear to ear. "I'm so glad you decided to come."

"I'm glad, too," she said. "I don't think anyone's ever been so happy to see me as Carmen here."

Alex grinned, stuffing his hands into the front pockets of his apron. "I'm not so sure about that."

He gestured for her to go ahead of him. "Kitchen's on your left, but you probably remember your way around. I hope it's okay that we're not using the dining room. It's covered in robot parts for something Eddie's working on."

It was more than okay. Gina felt guilty enough accepting a meal from him, not to mention possibly a place to stay. She wasn't much for fancy treatment and would be more comfortable in an informal setting anyway.

"Dinner's almost ready, but I can give you an

official tour of the cabin after." He turned to check her expression.

"I would love that."

She turned into the kitchen and spotted Eddie in the sunny breakfast nook, sitting at the same round walnut table where she'd enjoyed many meals as a young girl and as a teenager, and, more importantly, many precious conversations. *The most significant conversations in life often happen at kitchen tables*, she thought, a smile lifting the corners of her lips as a rush of happy memories flooded in.

Eddie looked up and gave a little wave, which Gina returned, before shifting his attention back to a notebook spread open in front of him. He bit his lip and resumed scribbling with a pencil.

"It's just us tonight," Alex said, pulling out a chair for her across from his nephew. "When I told Mom you were coming, she practically begged to join us, but I didn't want to overwhelm you." He grinned as Gina sat down. "You know how much she loves you, but if you're going to be in Peach Leaf for a while, I'm sure you'll have a chance to catch up."

Gina smiled uneasily over a sudden lump in her throat. "I'm sure we will. I hope she's doing okay."

"She is," Alex said, resting his palms on the

back of her chair. "After Dad passed, she moved from this house into a condo on Main Street, where she has a short walk to her favorite lattes and front-row seats to all the local gossip." He grinned. "She misses you. The whole family does."

Gina shifted so that she could face him where he stood behind her, having gently pushed in her chair. "Listen, Alex. I'm so sorry I wasn't here when… for the funeral. I wanted to come—regardless of things between us—but I was working overseas and by the time I heard the news from Sophie, I couldn't get a flight in time to make it. I should have tried harder—"

He shook his head. "Hey, it's okay. You don't owe us anything."

Though his statement was technically true, it bruised a little, and she deeply regretted not being there when Alex's family laid his brother and sister-in-law to rest.

"Is it dinnertime yet, Daddy?"

The air went still around them while Eddie, Alex and Gina all stared at Carmen, whose little round cheeks turned a dusty rose as a hand flew to her mouth.

"Oopsie! I mean Uncle Alex."

Alex looked down at the tiny girl by his side with

galaxies of love in his eyes. "It's okay, sweetheart," he said, tousling her hair.

"She does that a lot," Eddie said softly, before quickly returning his attention back to his notebook.

A beat of silence passed before Alex clapped his hands cheerfully. "Okay. To answer your question, mija, yes! Dinner is ready."

"Good, I'm sooo hungry!" Carmen responded, pulling herself up into the chair next to Gina's. After placing her magic wand next to her napkin and utensils, she rubbed her hands together and flashed a gap-toothed grin.

Gina giggled and Alex winked at her before disappearing into the kitchen, returning shortly with a large platter in each hand, which he set down with a waiter-like flourish.

"Oh, wow," Gina said, eyes wide at the delicious smells emanating from the table. "This looks amazing."

Alex pulled off his apron and draped it over the back of his chair, then sat down and began serving. "It's chickpea curry with basmati rice. Eddie's a vegetarian and I can't get enough Indian food these days, so we're kind of on a culinary adventure together. Isn't that right, Ed?"

Eddie nodded and Alex grinned as he filled Gina's plate. "He's my little foodie. He'll try anything new and he's got a very sophisticated palate, especially for a guy his age."

Gina's heart swelled with yearning to know more about this adorable little family, to catch up with the man at its helm, and, much to her surprise, to be part of it.

But she quickly brushed those feelings aside, knowing they had less to do with Alex and the kids specifically than they did about her own past. It wasn't the first time she'd wanted to be part of someone else's family. In fact, it happened almost every time she'd ever accepted an invitation to join a friend's Thanksgiving, Christmas, Hanukkah, birthday...you name it. She'd since learned it was a reaction to having grown up lonely, with no mom, aunts, uncles, or cousins—just one sibling to call her own. It was an ache that stemmed from a deep desire to be part of a family—a group of people who were supposed to love you unconditionally—who gathered together to celebrate life's joys and mourn its losses. And while she was always grateful to be included in her friends' family events, it wasn't quite the same as having her own.

The feeling would pass, eventually, and once again she'd remember why she usually spent holidays with a book and some takeout, which, let's be honest, were more reliable than some of the relatives other people had to deal with.

At least that's what Gina told herself, as Carmen chattered on about her day and her favorite TV show involving a cartoon aardvark and his friends. Eddie was quiet but seemed content, and Alex talked a little about the ranch as they all dug into a meal that tasted even better than the spicy scents of ginger, garam masala and turmeric had promised. Clearly, Alex had retained his childhood love of cooking, and further honed his skills over the years.

With a warm rush that caused her to focus intently on the napkin in her lap, Gina wondered what other skills he'd been honing in her absence.

"Is the food too spicy?" Alex asked, placing a hand over hers where it rested on the table, an action that only increased the flush of heat to her neck and face.

"No, no," she said, slipping her hand free as she forced herself to meet his eyes, hoping the blush had subsided. "The food is perfect."

Trying to cover up her emotions in front of a person who had known her so well would only make things worse. So she took a deep breath, faced her feelings head-on with as much bravery as she could muster and told the truth.

"Not only that, but you've taken such good care of this place," she said. "I can see the changes you've made, but it still feels like the home I always adored."

She felt him watching her as she glanced around the living area, updated since her last visit in tasteful shades of cobalt blue and eggshell, with Alex-y accents here and there. A marble and bronze coffee table, a rustic ladder bookcase filled with hardback mysteries and family photos, and a black lacquer chandelier. When she looked back at him, his eyes were soft with a touch of pride, and she sensed he was pleased that she approved of what he'd done with the Trevino family home.

She nodded toward the kids, who were absorbed in their food. "And in case you don't hear it enough, you're doing a great job here, Alex. I know it can't be easy, but you really are."

"Thank you," he said softly. "That means a lot."

A thousand unspoken things sparked in the air between them, until they both had to look away.

"Uncle Alex, I'm finished eating. Can I go and work on my robot?" Eddie asked.

"I want to come, too!" Carmen shouted, bouncing in her seat.

Alex looked at Eddie. "Do you mind if your sister joins you, kiddo?"

Eddie shook his head, and Gina thought she saw the slightest hint of a grin. "I don't mind," he said. "She can come."

"Yay!" Carmen added, making Gina and Alex laugh.

"Can I help clean up?" Gina asked, as Eddie took Carmen's hand and the siblings hurried off.

"Of course not. My mother would have my head if I let a guest help with dishes."

Gina giggled. "She would, wouldn't she?"

"Let me just put these in the dishwasher, and I'll be right back."

With that, he gathered their plates and utensils and stacked them on top of the platters with expert ease, and Gina had a sudden memory of him working summers at the grill in town, after long mornings helping his father and the ranch hands. Hard work was a Trevino family value, and Alex had always been full of restless energy, just like his niece.

Gina had once believed his restlessness would urge him to follow her from Peach Leaf, on to a bigger journey. But putting family first and commitment to his ancestors' land and livestock were an important part of his makeup too, outweighing his longing for adventure in the end, a fact she would do well to remember.

He returned from the kitchen a few moments later, took her hand and led her out the front door into a balmy evening filled with the sound of cicadas chirping and the creek running nearby. The sun wouldn't set for another hour but it rested behind a few clouds, casting a golden hue over the bluebonnets and Indian paintbrushes that dotted the unfenced yard in front of the main house.

"Will the kids be okay without you?" she asked.

Alex pulled a plastic object out of his pocket. "Baby monitor," he explained. "I've got them all over the house, along with cameras that would put the UK's CCTV to shame."

Gina chuckled as he led her down a limestone path bordered by solar lights.

"Things are different now than when we were young," he said. "Even in a small town, you can't be too careful. Plus Eddie is responsible beyond his age and seems to have an instinct for looking after Carmen. And I've taught him how to call 911 in case of an emergency. They should be okay for as long as it takes us to visit the cabin."

Gina nodded as they walked side by side, a gentle breeze tickling the strands of hair on her neck. "I remember when we were Eddie's age and your mom would shoo you out the door in the morning and not expect us to show up again until lunch-time."

"And you were always there to spend the day with me," he said. He paused, and his voice was lower when he spoke again. "Though I know part of that was because your dad wasn't the best at looking after you, and my mom was always re-lieved when he dropped you off with us on sum-mer mornings. I know she wanted to do the same for Sophie, too, but your sister preferred spending her days in the library among her books."

She nodded, her heart aching with those darker memories. Changing the subject, she said, "I had a good time at dinner. Eddie seems so smart and kind, and Carmen is sweet and accepting, even to a stranger like me."

"Sometimes I worry she's a little *too* accept-ing," Alex said.

"Being friendly isn't a bad thing, though," Gina countered.

"You're right. It's not. But I worry about her being out there in the world someday, off in the big city like you were. Or at college, Lord help me. With the parties, and the boys, and the parties *with* the boys, and—"

"Breathe, Alex," she said, stopping to put a hand

on his forearm. "You've got years before you need to worry about things like that."

He surprised her by actually taking her advice and inhaling deeply.

"Feel better?" she asked.

"Only a little." He glanced at her sideways with a grin.

They kept the house within view as they continued down the path, past a large rust-color barn, several chicken coops and a big greenhouse where Alex's mother had always nurtured a plethora of vegetables and flowers, the arrival of her precious seed catalogs each year one of the great joys of Mrs. Trevino's life. A few horses were wandering lazily around a pen, and cattle grazed freely in the nearest field.

"What about you?" he asked.

"Hmm?"

"What do you worry about these days?"

As they neared the bank of the creek, she pondered how to answer such a big question. Talking to him was easier than she could have imagined after all this time, and it would be so liberating to just open up and have someone besides Sophie to listen, and offer encouraging words or advice. But at what cost? How bad would it hurt to let him in, only to lose him all over again when she left?

Then again, he was here now. And he'd asked. Knowing Alex, he wouldn't have done so if he didn't truly intend to listen.

"Right now, my biggest worry is to figure out what to do with my life. I'm afraid I'll run out of savings before I can find another job, but I'm also afraid of taking something I don't want, just to make ends meet, staying too long, and getting trapped in a career I don't like for the rest of my life." A sigh escaped, and she relished the relief she felt at speaking the words aloud.

"That's big stuff," he responded.

"It is."

She appreciated that he hadn't brushed off her admission with platitudes to have faith or that everything would work out for the best. In the grand scheme of things, she was lucky. She had a roof over her head, enough to eat and she wasn't completely alone in the world. Things were worse for many. But that didn't mean she wasn't afraid of what the future held or didn't. She wasn't getting any younger, and, though she enjoyed teaching, she had done so on a contract basis while flitting around the globe, rather than in a school district with a pension plan. She hadn't built up the security that so many other people had by her age, and she could feel tension gripping her like a vise each time she thought about savings and retirement accounts and all those investment acronyms she didn't know the meaning of.

Even thinking about it made her hands shake and her mouth go as dry as the dirt around her. Alex had touched on a question she hadn't allowed herself to ask until now, too afraid to face the possible answers…

Is it too late to start over?

Chapter Five

The tremor in Gina's voice tugged at a locked-away place in Alex's heart.

This was the same woman he had once loved, but he saw bruises in her now that weren't there before. Places of hurt that might have been avoided if only he'd gone with her when she left for college.

Maybe that was just how things worked; life left marks, as he knew firsthand. But that didn't stop him from wondering if he could have shielded her from pain, the way he'd always tried to do when they were kids and she would come to school in her sister's hand-me-downs with set-in stains and unmended tears, and shoes with peeling-off soles.

Despite the economic distance between their

families, there'd been a connection between him and Gina from the moment they met as young children. His school friends, shallow with youth and privilege, hadn't understood why he was interested in Gina, but Alex didn't care, and neither did his family. It didn't matter to him that her clothes were off-brand and tattered, or that she didn't hang with the "right" crowd. What he'd seen then and what he saw now was kindness, hope and her own brand of beauty.

She was one of the bravest people he'd ever known, not least because of the challenges she'd faced growing up. He wasn't accustomed to seeing her defeated like this, and it caused anger, at whatever or whomever had stolen that grit from her, to simmer in his blood. He wanted to do something to help her get it back.

"Let's start at the simplest place," Alex suggested. "What do you love to do? What interests you so much that you would do it all day, every day if you had the chance?"

He thought it might take her a minute to answer, but she spoke so quickly it surprised him.

"If I could do anything I wanted, I'd turn my little upholstery repair business—and I use the term business very loosely—into a full-time career," she said.

He chuckled. "Your enthusiasm speaks for itself, Gina. If that's what you love, then that's what you should do with your life."

Tossing her head back, she let out a burst of laughter tinged with bitterness, another trait he didn't recognize in her. "It's a hobby, Alex, not a career. I could never make a living with my projects."

The negativity made him stop in his tracks. He turned to face her. "And why the hell not?"

She startled at his tone. "Um, because it's rare to make a living at any craft, and there's a lot of competition out there already, and I'd have to grow my business and build a hefty client list, and…"

"And, and, and…all I'm hearing are excuses for not going after your dream job."

He'd only meant to encourage her, but clearly he'd said the wrong thing. She glared at him, her eyes narrow and full of fire.

"I'm thankful for how nice you've been since I got back into town, and for the dinner and the cabin you're about to show me, Alex—" she hesitated "—but you don't have the right to give me advice on how to live my life."

The words sliced through layers and layers of skin he'd tried to thicken since she'd walked out; clearly, he hadn't done a good enough job. He'd fallen into place beside her as they'd walked his family's land and forgotten how much time had passed, and most importantly, that they weren't together anymore. They weren't even friends now, were they?

"You're right, Gina," he admitted. "I'm sorry I said that. It wasn't my place."

There were other things he wanted to say, of course. Things that were true but harsh, and it wasn't easy to bite his tongue. For all her incredible traits, for all the things he'd fallen in love with as a kid, Gina Heron had her faults. She was hard-headed, for one, and she had trouble accepting when she was wrong. But against all sense, he liked having her next to him. If she stuck around long enough, if she was open to listening, there would be time to rehash the past and air his own hard feelings about the way he'd been treated. Right now, though, all he wanted was for her to stay put.

She brushed a hand over her hair and dropped her head to stare at her feet. "It's okay. I shouldn't have lashed out. It's just a…rough subject. I guess I'm a little defensive about it these days." Glancing up, she looked off toward the creek. "I'd just like to see the cabin if that's okay."

He nodded. "Of course."

They walked on in silence until the cabin was

only a few yards ahead. He tried to look at it the way he imagined Gina would. It wasn't much, and she deserved better, but he would get it into shape if she said yes—an answer that mattered a lot more than he liked to admit.

They reached the simple log structure and walked up the steps to its wraparound porch—the cabin's best feature if you asked him. Before opening the door, which he made a mental note to lock from now on, Alex turned to meet Gina's eyes.

"We can drop the subject after this, but I want to go on record and say that you can do anything if you want to, Gina. You can make a living at your craft. I don't even have to see any evidence, because I know that if you love it, you'll work until you're amazing at it. You're the strongest woman I know—always have been—and the most stubborn."

"Hey!" she said, swatting his arm. But there wasn't any conviction behind it, and her eyes were smiling.

"I mean that in the best way possible," he said, serious as the summer sun. "You can do anything."

The smile was gone as quickly as it arrived, and the look that replaced it made him ache to reach out and pull her close.

"What if it *is* impossible, though?" she asked. "What if it's too late?"

Forgetting all the years behind them, Alex pushed through apprehension and the fear of being rejected, as he reached out to tuck a strand of hair behind her ear. She inhaled sharply as he placed a gentle finger just underneath her chin, lifting it until she met his eyes.

"This is something I'm sure of, Gina," he said, his heart pounding like a stampede of horses. "Life is too damn short, but it's never too late to change your path."

Her eyes shimmered with moisture, then she broke the tension with a mischievous grin. "Unless I want to be an Olympic gymnast," she joked. "Then it's probably a tiny bit late."

Though he responded by rolling his eyes, Alex was thankful for the lift in her mood, and that she'd lightened a heavy moment. Otherwise, he might have done something stupid, something he'd been burning to do since she'd set foot back in Peach Leaf, and kissed her. What kind of mess would that unleash in his and the kids' quiet little world?

It was fine to help out someone important from his past. It was even the right thing to do. But he'd stay far away from crossing that line into something else.

"Maybe so," he said. "But we both know you don't want to be a gymnast." He pulled the door open slowly. "And if you're going to build your business, you're going to need a quiet place to work, and that *is* something I can help with."

He moved aside, following closely as she took a few steps into the cabin.

"Like I said, it needs work. But it's got its merits."

If her wide eyes were any indication, Gina had already discovered some of them. She turned a little circle in place, gazing at a rectangular skylight cut into the ceiling, and the windows that covered nearly every wall. It was a humble space, dusty as hell at the moment, but his family didn't cut corners. His father, who had built the cabin himself, believed in doing every job the best it could be done. Dad had insisted the ranch hands were housed comfortably and well, and so it was. And now, against every instinct he had about keeping his heart shut off to her, Alex hoped Gina would see the beauty in that little house.

As if on cue, a ball of dust and probably dog fur tumbled across the bare hardwood floor.

If she noticed, Gina didn't mention it.

"I love it!" she said, clasping her hands in front of her chest.

Then, seeming to want to temper her display of excitement, she shoved her hands into her pockets and looked away. Clearing her throat, she spoke in a measured, serious tone. "I'm sure I won't be here long, but if it's still okay with you, I'll take it."

Alex offered what he hoped was an encouraging smile. "It's yours for as long as you need."

Alex and Gina returned to the main house to find Eddie and Carmen in the dining room, still immersed in Eddie's robot construction.

Gina stopped just outside the archway and stood quietly as she watched the kids. "Is it a school project?" she asked, glancing over her shoulder.

Alex shook his head, his lips tilting up at one corner. "It might be a little hard to believe, but no. He and Mom watched a show on PBS one afternoon about kids building robots, and that night he asked if he could do the same. The next day, we gathered up supplies and off he went."

"That's so cool," Gina replied in a mesmerized whisper.

"He's something else, that kid," Alex said, but his mind wasn't fully engaged in the conversation.

He knew it was dangerous to think along those

lines, but Gina looked so natural standing there in his home, watching the two little humans who now belonged to him. His head and heart went to places they didn't belong...

"Does Eddie know what he wants to be when he grows up?" she asked.

Alex was grateful she hadn't turned to catch him admiring the curve of her hip propped against the doorway, and the soft waves of hair that dipped over the collar of her shirt. The sudden, intense urge to move forward and wrap his hands around her waist nearly knocked the breath out of him.

How was it that she'd been his for so long, and now he had no claim to her at all? Couples broke up all the time, came and went from each other's lives as regularly as changing seasons...but not him and Gina. Their bond had been stronger and truer than anything he'd ever known. He would have bet everything on their staying together past gray hair and into whatever came next after life on earth.

If something like that could be broken, what in this world *could* he count on?

He looked up to find her eyes filled with concern.

"You okay?" she asked.

He nodded. "Does anyone really know what they

want to be when they grow up?" he said, in response to her question about Eddie.

"Good point," Gina answered. "I certainly
thought I had everything figured out—" she
pushed out a breath "—and look at me now."

Her words hung heavy in the air, and he wanted
to soothe her, to make her understand that he believed in her and knew, even if she didn't, that she
could do anything she set her mind to. But that
wasn't his place, as she'd made so clear only moments before.

"Seriously though, it just depends on the day.
Sometimes he wants to be a rocket scientist or an
astronaut, other days it's a geologist or a robotics
engineer or a paleontologist." The memory made
him smile. "That was a fun one. The house was
covered in dinosaur books for weeks, and all Eddie
could talk about was digging in the front yard to
see if we might be sitting on a pile of fossils."

Gina turned to look at him, her mouth open as
if about to speak, when Carmen spotted her.

"Miss Gina!" she shouted, waving the magic
wand as she jumped down from the chair next to
Eddie. Her brother looked up at the noise, calmly
setting down an LED light and battery.

"Hey, Carmen!" Gina greeted, as Alex's niece

ran up to hug her knees. "Hey, Eddie," she called. "How's the project coming?"

Eddie held out a hand and twisted it from side to side. "Okay," he said.

Alex curbed the urge to grin at his nephew's mannerisms. Eddie was ten going on forty, and sometimes Alex had to remind himself that, despite Eddie's maturity and the tragedy he'd endured at such a young age, he was indeed still a kid. Parenting such a unique person came with challenges...when to be physically affectionate and when to give space, when to talk and when to listen, when to push and when to hold back.

It was easier with Carmen, who instinctively asked for what she needed in terms Alex could understand: open arms, tears, outbursts of joy and sadness.

The two kids couldn't have been more different.

Had he been able to predict the future, he would have asked his brother and sister-in-law all the questions he had about how to raise these children. He had no idea, back then, how little he knew and how much would be required of him.

It surprised him to find that he wanted to share all of this with Gina, but he'd seen how uncomfortable she was during story time in the bookstore, and he didn't want to freak her out by loading her down with heavy parenting concerns.

"Uncle Alex, can Miss Gina stay for story time?" Carmen asked, still hugging Gina's legs. "I want her to read the princess parts. You don't do it right."

Gina reached up to cover her mouth, but a bubble of laughter escaped nonetheless.

"Hey," Alex protested. "I thought I was a pretty good princess!" He turned to Gina. "Everyone's a critic."

Her eyes met his, and he picked up on her obvious hesitation.

"Maybe another time," he said, to much outcry from Carmen. Even Eddie's shoulders seemed to drop. "Miss Gina probably has other things to do besides hang out with us all night." Putting a hand up to shield his mouth, he whispered playfully, "This is your chance to escape a *very* long bedtime routine. Trust me."

Then he reached down to pick up Carmen, who had attached herself to their guest like a tiny, purple-clad barnacle. Instead of looking relieved, Gina's expression was regretful, her fingers gently tousling Carmen's curls when he lifted away his niece.

"Another time," she echoed softly.

* * *

Gina pushed back bittersweet memories as Alex waved goodbye from the front porch, then she looked away quickly rather than watch Trevino Ranch fade in the rearview mirror of her old Subaru.

Her heart bubbled with emotion as she pulled through the front gate and onto the road that would take her back into Peach Leaf and the safety of Sophie's cozy little home above the bookstore. She chose a classic rock station and turned the music up loud, doing her best to drown out a surge of nostalgia.

He might have made a few changes to the house, and he was now a father figure, but little else had changed about Alex. He remained the kind, hardworking, steady man she once thought she would marry, and much to her astonishment, her feelings for him had changed far less than she'd believed.

Which made things…complicated, seeing as she'd just agreed to live on his land. He would be nearby, all the time, and unless she wanted to exist like a hermit, she would have to face him every day.

Him and those adorable little kids.

What have I gotten myself into? she thought.

Looking up, she realized she'd missed the turn

that would have taken her straight into town. Instead, she found herself on the outskirts of Peach Leaf, just up the road from the apartment building where she'd spent the last three years of high school—the longest her father had ever kept their little family in one place.

A deserted gas station and a long-abandoned discount store were the only other buildings close by. Gina stopped the car, closed her eyes and breathed deeply. Then she opened her eyes and pulled forward, rolling to a stop just outside the small apartment complex.

From the car, she could see that time had not been friendly to the U-shaped trio of two-story buildings, and the low-quality siding had rotted in places that no one was coming to fix. The lawn, mostly weeds, was sparse and unkempt, and the little concrete fountain out front, no doubt intended to be cheerful, sprouted a weak stream of greenish water. Other than the wear of years gone by, not much had changed.

A twinge of guilt filled her as it always did when she thought about that place, and about the life she, Sophie and her mostly absent father had lived there, constantly aware that things could have been much worse.

But that didn't mean her pain wasn't real, and

she felt the sting of tears at the backs of her eyes as she recalled those tough days at school and the quiet, empty unit she and Sophie had come back to…those long afternoons that seemed to stretch on forever after their homework was done. Dinner wasn't guaranteed, there wasn't money for cable, and she and Sophie had read nearly everything at the library.

Gina had been so happy to get away from there. So grateful for the few scholarships she'd managed to stitch together on her own, with very little help from the underfunded school district and its one overwhelmed counselor.

And yet her sister stayed. Somehow, Sophie had let go of their difficult past and made a home of her own in Peach Leaf. The bookstore was successful, Sophie kept old friends and made new, and she had a community of people who cared about her. Sophie was surrounded by a family of her own creation, whereas Gina, despite the joy she'd found in teaching and traveling, had always been something of a loner.

Until recently, this hadn't bothered her. But being back here, seeing Sophie thrive and Alex settling into his new roles…

She'd given up searching for a home long ago, but now something stirred in her, and she wondered if that universal desire for belonging had returned. Could she do what her sister had done? Could she put the past behind her and find a way forward that didn't involve running forever?

From somewhere deep in her purse, Gina's phone buzzed. Pulled from her thoughts, she reached into the bag and fumbled around, grabbing the device just in time to catch the last ring.

"Sophie?" Gina answered. "What's up?"

"Where are you?" Sophie asked, her voice high-pitched with worry. "I thought you'd be back from dinner by now. I'm ready for ice cream, and I'm dying to hear how it went!"

Gina took a last glance at the old apartment complex before turning away. "Just taking a quick trip down memory lane. Don't worry," she said. "I'll be home soon."

Chapter Six

When Alex walked into the coffee shop on Main Street a few mornings later, an onslaught of excited female voices erupted from the far corner of the room. Everyone in the café turned briefly, probably expecting Idris Elba or someone equally famous to stroll through the door, rather than a local rancher. Feeling his cheeks grow warm at the unnecessary attention, Alex removed his cowboy hat and smiled sheepishly at the barista before placing his order, bracing himself for what he knew would be a highly energetic encounter for such an early hour.

"Mijo!" his mother, Rosa, called out loudly enough so that everyone within a mile of the café could hear. Her arms, brown and toned from container gardening on the patio of her condo, and yoga in Peach Leaf Park, waved wildly above a crown of black curls. "Come and sit with us!"

Alex obliged, partly because he loved his mom, of course, but also because if he didn't, he knew her loyal group of friends would never let him live it down.

"Hi, Mom. Hello, ladies," he said with a nod.

He glanced around at the four women surrounding Rosa Trevino in a deep-green leather booth. Estelle, Sandy, Quita, and Janine were almost as familiar to him as his own aunts, and as soon as he borrowed a chair from a nearby table and sat down, they made quick work of catching him up on everything that had happened since he'd last seen them, only the week before. And—to no one's surprise—they knew not only that Gina had been to dinner at the ranch a few nights ago, but that she might soon become a resident of Alex's cabin.

"So, does this mean the two of you are thinking of getting back together?" Janine asked, hazel eyes shining behind a pair of glittery amethyst bifocals.

"Hush, Janine!" Quita admonished, lightly swatting the woman next to her. "He doesn't have to tell us that." Quita rolled dark brown eyes at her friend, right before leaning in to Alex and adding,

"Unless he wants to, that is." She flashed a hopeful smile and he couldn't help but laugh.

"I always did love that girl," chimed in Sandy, blue eyes sparkling under a wave of blond bangs. "She was a quiet one, but sweet as honey and smart as a whip. I'm not surprised she went off and became a teacher, though I think we all wished you two had gotten hitched." She took a sip of her whipped-cream topped beverage and regarded him warmly.

Alex swallowed and met his mom's sympathetic gaze. She patted his knee under the table.

"Well, that's all water under the bridge, isn't it?" said Quita, winking. "Gina's home now and that's what matters."

Quita always had been his favorite, Alex thought with a grin.

"What is she up to these days, dear?" Estelle asked, cutting a chocolate-chip muffin into two pieces. Her slender wrists jingled with colorful bracelets as she slid half over to Alex on a napkin.

Alex accepted the fluffy confection with a thank-you, and took a deep breath before speaking. "That's an interesting question," he began.

After dropping Eddie and Carmen at school, he'd spent the short drive over trying to figure out how best to help Gina. He would need to tread carefully to avoid overstepping his bounds and running the risk of her shutting down, but he had an idea that was sure to work.

Between them, his mom, Estelle, Quita, Sandy and Janine knew every person and proprietor in town. If he mentioned Gina's dreams for her business, the five women would have her booked solid with projects to fill her calendar for the next year, and, while she would probably be pleased to have the work, he didn't want to overwhelm Gina or make her feel like he'd given her a handout. She had grown up economically disadvantaged while Alex came from a legacy of successful ranchers and old family money. Though he would have loved her no matter what, and had never cared about material things, his family's generosity toward her had always been a point of contention between them. He was very aware that in Gina's way of thinking, only a fine line stood between a gift from a lover and what she interpreted as unwanted charity.

Then again, that's how things worked in Peach Leaf; people looked out for one another. So, if Alex had the resources to give Gina's business a boost, he'd be wrong not to do so.

He took a bite of his muffin half and looked up into five pairs of eagerly waiting eyes.

"She's started her own business restoring up-holstery," he said finally, to a chorus of admiring noises and comments. "As well as doing custom work to order."

"Beth mentioned that she needs a new set of chairs for the reading area in the library," Quita said, pausing to take a sip of her coffee. "But the budget won't cover a brand-new set, so reuphol-stering the ones they already have would definitely be a better move."

"My friend Henrietta has an antique couch passed down from her great-grandmother. There's a big ole tear in one of the cushions that needs to be repaired," added Sandy, spreading her arms wide to indicate the size of the rip.

Janine waved jazz hands excitedly. "Oh! Sarah at the community center wants to redo—"

"Okay, ladies, okay," Alex's mom chided, rais-ing her palms to quiet her friends. "I'm sure if we put our heads together, we can all think of projects for Gina, but we don't want to scare the poor girl right out of town!"

"I hear that," said Estelle.

"You're right," Janine agreed.

"Thank you," Alex said. "I appreciate your ideas so much, and I will definitely need you to spread the word around town, but we should probably start small and let Gina set the pace." He smiled around the table. "I know she'll be excited, but she's got her work cut out for her, moving into the cabin, and she'll need time to set up a workspace before she takes on projects."

His mom nodded, and he knew they were on the same page. In no time, Gina would have the work she needed, but he could trust Rosa to make sure the word-of-mouth spread didn't move too fast or spin out of control like a wildfire.

"Okay, girls. Let's let Alex get on with his day and we'll make a plan," his mom suggested, and everyone reached into their purses to pull out notebooks and pens.

Alex teased the ladies for operating like a hive of bees, but his heart swelled with love and gratitude as he sipped his coffee quietly, watching the women around the table, knowing they would do anything to help a community member—a label Gina carried whether she wanted it or not. It didn't matter that she'd fled town years ago and barely looked back. Peach Leaf was in her bones, and the people who cared about her—of which there were more than she knew—would do whatever they could at the drop of a hat to help turn her dreams into reality.

Maybe if he could do a better job of showing her that this time, Gina wouldn't be in such a hurry to run again.

* * *

"Is Miss Gina really going to live here?" Carmen asked, the words bouncing behind her as she skipped along the wildflower-lined path toward the cabin.

A corner of Alex's mouth turned up at the thought. "Yes, she is. At least for a little while." He frowned and bit his lip as Carmen almost tripped, correcting her footing just in time. "Be careful, Carmen. Don't get too far ahead of me and Eddie."

"Goodie, goodie, goodie!" she called, seemingly unconcerned about nearly falling. "That means we can visit her every day."

Eddie shook his head, causing Alex to chuckle. "No, we can't visit her every day, sweetheart," he said to Carmen. She's got her own life and her own business to run, and she'll need time and quiet to do that. We don't want to overload her."

"But we'll get to visit sometimes, though, right?" Eddie asked in a soft tone, his brown eyes squinting in the sun as he stared up at his uncle.

Startled by the question, and by the touch of eagerness in it, Alex paused a few seconds before answering.

Though his nephew was kindhearted and generous, Eddie didn't warm quickly to just anyone. This indication that he was fond of Gina was encouraging…but also worrisome. What if Eddie developed an attachment to her, only to find himself hurt and confused when she left again?

"Of course we will, buddy," he said, briefly squeezing Eddie's shoulder, then thought better of it, not wanting his words to sound like a promise he might not be able to keep. "If she invites us over, we'll visit."

He reached over to put an arm around Eddie, and was beyond happy when his nephew molded into Alex's side. The experience of having these kids in his life was a blessing he cherished even more now that they lived with him full-time. There were moments when the weight of his responsibility took his breath away, but other times, being with them was sheer joy.

As they neared the cabin, Alex's excitement began to build. Only a week had passed, but the guys were working fast to get the cabin into shape for Gina. Alex's cousin Jesse had begun to ease into his role as a contractor. Because the cabin needed new plumbing and wiring rather than just a surface-level remodel, Jesse was getting a chance to stretch his wings. He still had a way to go before he'd be able to handle bigger jobs, but his portfolio was growing quickly and he was on his way to becoming an excellent builder.

Alex liked the idea that helping his cousin's business would give Gina the space to build her own, and because Jesse hired talented workers and treated them well, the work was guaranteed to be high quality.

"Hey, there you are!" Jesse called out as Alex and the kids came into view of the cabin. "How are my little monsters?"

Carmen ran into Jesse's arms and Eddie walked up calmly for a quick high five before resuming his spot at Alex's side. "How's it going, Jess?" Alex said, accepting his cousin's fist bump.

"Couldn't be better," Jesse said, tickling a giggly Carmen before setting her back on the ground. "We're on track to finish a day early." He caught Alex's eye and grinned. "I know that'll make your girl happy."

"She's not my girl and you know it," Alex protested, sounding pathetically unconvincing even to his own ears.

"Whatever you say, man," Jesse responded, shaking his head. "Anyway, go on in and take a look. There's an extra hard hat on the porch rail, and I'll be right behind you."

"Always a stickler for safety," Alex teased, though he wouldn't have it any other way.

"You know it." Jesse flashed the million-watt

smile that had earned him something of a reputation around town for being a ladies' man, though Jesse had confided in Alex that he'd always wanted what his cousin had with Gina growing up. Little had they known then that even things that looked perfect on the outside had the potential to fall apart. Hopefully, Alex thought, gazing at the cabin's freshly varnished exterior, the same wouldn't be true for this place.

He grabbed a couple of hard hats and put one on Eddie's head while Jesse did the same for Carmen. Ill-fitting though it was, he fastened the straps under his nephew's chin before donning his own.

With Eddie just behind him, Alex jogged up the steps and ran his hand along the glazed porch railing, which proved as glossy under his touch as it appeared. Unbidden, an image popped into his head: him wrapping garland around that same railing while Gina stood nearby, smiling and sipping hot chocolate. The two of them decorating a tree with shining colorful lights, then snuggling up together on a couch to admire their work before things heated up. Gina's hair tumbling down out of its band, her legs wrapped around him as he lifted her from the couch to carry her into...

"So what do you think?" Jesse asked loudly, pulling Alex from what could only be called a fantasy. An embarrassing fantasy he shouldn't be having.

He arranged his features as quickly as possible before his cousin had a chance to figure him out. Alex and Jesse had grown up together, and it wouldn't take much to see right through him. Plus it was warm in the cabin, the new AC system not yet installed.

"Hey, are you all right?" Jesse asked again, placing a hand on Alex's shoulder. Eddie stared up at him too, waiting for an answer.

"Yeah, yeah, fine," Alex responded, shaking off his cousin's concerned gesture. "Just a little light-headed from the heat in here. It's like a sauna."

Jesse's eyes narrowed. "The rancher, who spends all day outside, most days of the year, in *Texas*, is too hot." His worried expression shifted into a mischievous grin. "You were thinking about *her* just now, weren't you?"

"I wasn't," Alex said, scrubbing a hand over his late afternoon stubble. He didn't say more because it would only make things worse. Everyone in his entire family had been upset after Alex and Gina broke up, including Jesse. They'd loved her and wanted to see her join their family permanently. So of course they were all looking for signs that the high school sweethearts might rekindle a smothered flame and revive that plan for a future that included their beloved Gina. Even his mom's coffee shop posse had expressed the same sentiment just that morning.

"Riiight," Jesse said, obviously not believing his cousin.

Alex lifted his chin in defiance. He'd have to try harder not to give the Trevino clan any unrealistic hope, including himself.

"It's incredible, Jess," he said, meaning the words, and hoping they would suffice to change the subject. "You guys have done an amazing job here."

"Well, this is just the living area," Jesse replied, temporarily placated and beaming from the compliment as he lifted Carmen onto his shoulders. "Wait till you see the rest. Gina's gonna love it so much she'll never want to leave!"

As Eddie followed Jesse from the living area into the bedroom, Alex rubbed his eyes and released a heavy sigh.

So much for letting go of unrealistic hope.

The following week found Gina leaning against the checkout counter of Peach Leaf Pages, waiting anxiously for the doorbell to chime.

"You know what they say about a watched pot," Sophie said, emerging from the back of the bookshop with two dusting rags, one of which she handed to her sister. Sophie's hair swung behind her in a ponytail, and a red bandanna circled her crown. She always made use of slow times in the store for cleaning, a habit Gina noticed early on and did her best to avoid by offering to run errands. But this morning, there was no escape.

"Yeah, but *they*—" Gina made bunny-ear quotations with her fingers "—never said anything about a watched *door*," she teased.

"Same thing," Sophie called, rolling her eyes. "That's why it's a proverb, silly." She headed for the reading corner and began wiping down an accent table and lamp. "Besides, standing sentry isn't necessary when it comes to Alex. He wouldn't miss a date with you unless an emergency happened, and you know that, so you're only going to make yourself nervous staring out that window."

"It's not a date, I hasten to add, but you've got a point," Gina said, taking her own rag, which Sophie had apparently moistened with lemon-scented polish, and starting on a set of shelves as far away from the front door as possible.

"Sometimes your big sis is wise," Sophie responded. "Wise beyond my years, I mean, since I'm not exactly an old sage."

"Yet," Gina added, sticking out her tongue.

"Hey, watch it!"

Sophie plunged toward Gina, threatening to use her dirty dust rag as a weapon. When the bell jangled only a few seconds later, it surprised them both.

"What did I tell you?" Sophie asked with a cheeky wink.

Gina shot her a look and went to join Alex at the front, dropping the rag behind the desk and wiping her hands on her jeans along the way.

"Hey," Alex greeted as she neared him.

He waved to Sophie who waved back, Gina noticed, with far too much enthusiasm.

Alex's hair was damp, probably from a recent shower. If he was the same Alex she'd always known, he would have been up with the dawn and put in a full day's work before the clock struck noon. The ends of his dark locks curled slightly with the moisture, and she ached to run her hands through the strands like she had in bygone days. The edges just reached the collar of his dark blue T-shirt. As always, he wore soft, faded jeans and a worn pair of cowboy boots, but Gina was smart enough not to let her eyes linger too long on his bottom half. If she did, the color in her cheeks would reveal every conflicting emotion pulsing through her brain.

"Hey, yourself," she said, returning his smile.

When he'd called a few days ago to let her know that the cabin was finished—*her* cabin, he'd said— Gina had only just begun to realize that this…situation…was going to be very real, very soon. It had only gotten more real when he'd called again last night to ask if she wanted to come shopping with him to pick out a few pieces of furniture and curtains for the bedroom—which was large, having once housed bunks for ranch hands—and front windows.

"I haven't changed my mind since we talked yesterday. I still think this is a bad idea," she said, her voice catching a little with nerves. "You've done plenty just by offering me a place to stay. I definitely don't think you should be furnishing it for me as well." Her tone dropped an octave. "I'm not a charity case anymore, you know."

His cheeks filled with color at her last statement, and she immediately wished she could take it back. A flicker of pain briefly shaded his expression.

"I know that, Gina."

He stepped closer and held out an open hand, as if wanting to fold hers inside it. She picked up the signature scent of cinnamon and was instantly transported to a time when he was hers, when she could act on every instinct to pull his mouth close and cover it with her own.

"I've always known that. But I promised you a furnished cabin, and that's what I'm going to give you. I don't go back on my word."

His face was only inches away now, and his eyes bore into hers with a tender ferocity. His promise seeped deep into her bones, washing over her and calming the anxiousness she seemed to carry everywhere these days. Trust rose up within her and she felt prompted to give him her hand; he wrapped his fingers around hers. Her heart beat so quickly she was certain if she tried, she'd barely be able to utter a sound, but any sound was better than standing there in silence like a total doofus with Sophie watching them both as if she'd stumbled upon a movie set.

Gina cleared her throat. "I'll come with you, on one condition."

Alex raised a brow and his lips turned up in a grin. "You're making demands now?"

Tilting up her chin, Gina responded, "I am."

That grin broke into a full, shining smile that instantly had her heart going even faster.

"All right, name your price."

"Okay. I don't want to go to a regular furniture store," she said.

Alex's eyes widened but he remained quiet, letting her speak.

"There's a flea market going on today. I'd rather go to that if you don't mind." Biting her lip, she waited for his response.

"Sure thing, Gina, but don't look at me if you come home to find a live animal's made a nest under the sofa cushions."

"Hey!" Laughing, she released his hand to give him a good swat on the shoulder, which he expertly dodged. "Seriously, though. I've gotten really good at picking out older pieces and making them new again." She paused, and he watched her intently. "It's not that I don't like new stuff, but older items often have more character. They've lived a little, and I feel like they carry stories with them. I really love pairing an old piece with new fabric and giving it a second chance."

Still meeting her eyes, Alex took her hand again and squeezed it gently. "Second chances seem to be a favorite theme of yours, don't they?"

Gina's heart skipped and her throat tightened around anything she might have said, but Alex just nodded and led her to the front door.

"Come on," he said, winking. "There's a flea market waiting for us."

* * *

People said everything was bigger in Texas, and the weekly Peach Leaf Outdoor Market was no exception.

It had been years since she'd been back in town long enough to attend, and plenty had changed. The stalls stretched out for a quarter mile on both sides of a center walkway, and Gina noticed that pretty much all the vendors now had portable electronic card readers instead of the old all-cash system she was used to from childhood. But the quality of the goods was no different. The market's only rule was: "don't sell anything you wouldn't give to a friend," and everyone who showed up took it very seriously, which made it an absolutely amazing place to find used treasures.

"Isn't it awesome?" she asked Alex as he opened the passenger door of his truck to help her down. The sun was shining in a cloudless blue sky, and the heat of the day was still hours away. A surge of anticipation rushed through her.

She'd always had a thing for fabric and furniture, and Rosa Trevino had taught her how to sew when she was a teen. Gina knew the skill had been given to her for practical reasons, so that she could mend her own worn garments to get the bullies at school off her back. Sadly, it hadn't helped in that regard, but she'd kept practicing and taking classes whenever she could, eventually honing in on simple upholstery repair, and then, at the behest of a few friends, doing her own custom work. There were few things in the world that brought her more pleasure than joining an old item with just the right textile and giving it new life. Alex was right—she did love a second chance.

Another thing she loved was that he noticed this about her.

He *saw* her.

"I'll have to take your word for it," he said, squinting. "I haven't been here since Mom dragged me a time or two as a kid, until I learned how to get out of it by volunteering to mend fences with Dad."

"Really? You didn't have to say yes to this, you know." Gina grinned mischievously.

"Oh, didn't I? If I remember correctly, your one condition of joining me to shop for your cabin was that we couldn't go to an actual, real store." He shot her a faux glare.

"This is a real store, my friend. You're just not seeing its potential." She stretched out her arms, bare in a kelly green tank top. The sun's rays tickled her skin with the promise of a gorgeous, early-fall day. "Look around at all the possibilities."

"Look around at all the—"

Gina put a hand over his mouth, surprising the heck out of him. "Don't you dare say *junk*, Alex Trevino. Don't you even dare!"

Gripping her fingers, he tugged them gently away. "I wasn't going to say…*that word*," he teased.

She stared up at him, his brown eyes twinkling in the soft midmorning light.

He was looking at her the same way he always had, as if not a second had passed. With tenderness, humor, admiration. With…love.

Suddenly, the laughter, the lightheartedness of the moment threatened to turn darker as doubts began to fill her mind. What was she doing here? Why had she said yes to a cabin she didn't deserve? On land that belonged to the love of her life, a man she'd walked away from without a backward glance? Who was she to say yes to this strange but promising new beginning?

Digging up a dormant store of strength from somewhere deep inside, Gina shook her head and pushed past the negative self-talk that had become such a constant, unwanted companion over the past few months. If Sophie could hear Gina's thoughts, she would remind her sister that Gina was a person, worthy of love and companionship if she wanted them. Worthy of joy and happiness.

If only it were as easy to believe as it was to hear.

Chapter Seven

"So, where should we go first?" Alex asked, earning a sideways look from Gina.

"You don't *plan* at a flea market, Alex."

She paused, closed her eyes and pulled in a deep breath, then she opened them again.

"You listen, and let inspiration find *you*."

Now it was her turn to get the side-eye.

"What the heck does that mean?"

"I can't speak for you," she said, "but for me, it means I'm going to keep my mind open and see if anything speaks to me."

"I'm all for having an open mind," he said, keeping his tone light, "but if the furniture starts talking to me, I'm going to have to ask you to call a doctor."

It pleased him when she reached up a hand to stifle a laugh. God, how he'd missed that sound. That perfect joy bubbling out from someone he adored.

Listening to that musical noise, he made a spur-of-the-moment deal with himself. After this day out with Gina, he'd go back to keeping his distance, to putting the kids' needs first, to ignoring the feelings that kept threatening to take over his body when Gina was around. Tomorrow, he'd lock up the part of him that still wanted her despite the fact she didn't fit into the life he had now as sole parent of two precious kids. But today, with a breathtaking blue sky and the sun shining and the whole afternoon ahead of them, he'd allow himself to live in the moment. Just for one day, he would pretend like nothing had ever broken between them, like they were still two teenagers in love… like she'd never left and taken his heart with her.

With that vow in place, and the clock ticking, he looked at her, really *looked* at her for the first time since she'd shown back up in their hometown.

Her wheat-colored curls were encircled by a yellow fabric headband and her bare shoulders, which he knew from experience would be pink from the sun by the end of the day, were sprinkled with freckles that he wanted to kiss one by one. When she turned to meet his gaze, her eyes were filled with all the things he loved about her—intelligence, humor, curiosity—and he gave over to the insistent urge to soak it all in, on the chance she'd leave again and he would have to pull this image of her from his memory for the rest of his life.

"Really, though," she said, reaching out a tentative hand, which he eagerly accepted. "Let's just walk and see if we find anything worth a closer look."

She stared down at their hands, and he caught the hint of a smile before she looked back up at the booths ahead.

"Okay, I'm all centered and ready to find something amazing," he said, knowing this would please her. He released her hand, rubbed his hands together, and then clapped once. "Let's do this."

"Yes!" she shouted, pumping a fist, and they both laughed like two excited kids racing into a theme park on the first day of summer break.

They walked down the gravel path, shaded by old live oaks and the canvas-covered wood frames of the booths. Their first stop was a used-book stand, and after only five minutes of browsing, Gina had three age-yellowed historical romances from the nineties to take home to Sophie, and Alex had the latest volume in a mystery series he loved.

"I can't believe it," he said. "This is brand-new and I'm only out five bucks!"

"Um, *yeah*, that's the beauty of the flea market," she declared flatly, as if this was the most obvious thing anyone had ever said. "The previous owner probably enjoys the experience of cracking open a brand-new hardback but doesn't want it taking up space on a bookshelf, so they bought it and didn't want to keep it after reading."

"I'll have to do this more often," he said, glancing at her as they paid for their books and thanked the seller. "And Van will love this one, too, so I can pass it along when I'm done."

"Perfect," Gina said, pulling a canvas shopping bag out of her purse. "Here, I'll carry those."

Alex handed over his purchase and they left the stall, making their way through a growing crowd back to the center path.

"So, how long have you and Van been friends?" she asked, eyes on her blue-painted toenails.

Why the sudden shyness? he wondered silently. But an answer followed almost immediately.

Perhaps it was painful for her to think about life moving on in Peach Leaf after she'd gone, especially for those people she'd cared for like him and Sophie. She must have known he would continue to live his life without her—meet new people, make new friends—but it couldn't be easy to

think about what she'd left behind, even if it had
been her decision.

"Um, let me see. If I recall correctly, she and
Darian moved here right around the time Eddie was
born, and we became friends a couple years later,
so eight years ago or so. Van opened the craft shop
right away, and Darian helped her get it set up and
then started his accounting business shortly after."

Gina glanced at the stalls while they walked,
worrying her lower lip as she assessed each one,
always giving a friendly wave when she passed
the proprietor. He wondered what sort of magic
she was looking for in a piece of furniture, what
would make something stand out to her. Everything about her fascinated him, just as it always
had. The adventures she'd been on, her active, cre-
ative mind, her body… It occurred to him that she
might have new scars, marks on her skin and on
her soul from experiences she'd had without him—
some of which he didn't want to think about.

"She seems really lovely," Gina said. "It was
good of her to be so kind to me when we met, especially since she must know our history, and might
judge me for breaking your…for our breakup."

Alex shot her a glance. "Well, I don't think Van
is capable of unkindness," he said. "But I also
know she has good taste in people. She can tell a

good human from a rotten one, and whatever you and I had in the past, Gina, you are definitely a good person. One of the best."

She turned briefly and opened her mouth to speak, then closed it and gave him a tight-lipped smile as they walked on. He stifled the need to ask her what she was going to say. There was a time when the words would have come without thinking, but things were different now. If she wanted to say something to him, he was more than ready to listen, but he wasn't going to push.

After passing a few stalls offering children's toys and games, Gina paused and backtracked a few steps as if her flea market dowser had given her a tug.

"Something got your senses tingling?" Alex asked.

"Maybe." She raised her brows and flashed him a grin. "Only one way to find out."

He followed her into a stall filled wall-to-wall with old furniture, some of which had clearly seen better days. Left to his own devices, Alex would have tipped his hat at the vendor and sauntered right out of there. His tastes tended toward what his cousin Jesse jokingly called "cowboy chic." New, modern furniture and minimalist decor in muted blues and grays, textures and colors that made him feel calm and comfortable after hard days outside surrounded by sunshine and Texas bluebonnets. But his curiosity was piqued because Gina's was, so he kept his opinions to himself and stood back, watching with interest as she perused the stall.

"Oh, would you look at this?" Gina stage-whispered.

In all of two footsteps he joined her on the other side of the stall where she stared, wide-eyed as a kid at Christmas, at the ugliest damn chair he'd ever seen. Not wanting to burst whatever bubble the thing had inspired in Gina, he quickly schooled his features into an expression he desperately hoped did *not* relay his true feelings.

She beamed up at him. "Isn't it marvelous?"

"Um, ye-es," he stammered before catching himself. "Yes! It's…amazing!"

Seeing right through this malarkey, Gina pressed her lips together and put a hand over her mouth, but he heard the giggle she tried to stifle.

"Really?" she asked, eyes narrowed and arms crossed. "You love it?"

Rosa Trevino had taught her children that if they couldn't say something nice, they shouldn't say anything at all, so Alex thought it best to keep a lid on it. He nodded with way too much vigor.

Gina tilted her head back and laughed. "I'm just messing with you," she said, reaching out to tickle his side before he could duck out of reach. It was a move that, in former days, had often led to her running away and him catching her, lifting her over his head and taking her off to…

He shoved the thought aside before it got out of hand, but Gina must have seen straight into his heart. Color flushed up her neck and into her freckled cheeks and she quickly looked away, clearing her throat.

"Anyway, it's not much right now, but that will change once I get it home and give it some TLC." With a gleam in her eyes, she reached out to caress the chair's back. "I've got just the right fabric to pair with this rich cedar. I'll just strip this old finish, give it a good sanding, and—"

"You're the first person who hasn't walked past that chair with their nose in the sky," called a boisterous voice behind them.

Uh-oh, Alex thought.

He knew that voice. So did Gina.

This wasn't good.

Gina turned around slowly, and the color drained from her face the second she saw the owner of the husky tenor.

"Kacey?" Gina whispered.

Kacey Carlisle stopped abruptly. Her mouth dropped open but no words came out.

The two women stared at each other for what felt like an hour, or at least long enough for sweat to bead under Alex's hat and run down his neck in a rivulet. But whatever he was feeling wouldn't hold a candle to his companion's.

Because Kacey Carlisle and her posse had made high school a living hell for Gina.

Gina's mouth went dry, and the hairs on the back of her neck stood at attention.

The morning had been going so well. So, so well. Better than she could have imagined.

Until she'd turned around and found herself face-to-face with one of the last people on earth she ever wanted to see again.

Of course she'd known this was a possibility. *Of course* she'd thought about what she might say if it happened. But the fact was, that now, in the middle of it, all those words escaped her.

Pulling in a deep breath, Gina went through a list of things around her, to ground her in the present. Gravel under her feet. Canvas tent above her. Neglected chair with lots of potential in front of her. Alex by her side.

Alex, who had been by her side back in school,

defending her the last time Kacey and company had gotten their kicks by hurting her, as he had all the other times too.

Alex, who stood right next to her even now, watching her closely. Somewhere in the last minute or so, he had come closer and his hand had gone to the small of her back, where it still rested. She knew instinctively that he was giving her room to speak, offering his quiet strength while she took agency over what they all knew was an awkward situation.

She closed her eyes.

Time had passed, Gina reminded herself. She wasn't an insecure kid anymore. Sure, she might not have built the life she wanted just yet, and she might not be perfect—she *definitely* wasn't perfect—but she had a kind heart and an open mind. And she knew enough to know that people could change.

At least she hoped they could.

She opened her eyes and Kacey was still standing there, nervously gripping a clipboard and pen.

"Alex," Kacey greeted, nodding.

"Kacey." His voice was firm.

"Hey, Gina," Kacey said, meeting her stare. "It's been a while."

Gina took a deep breath. "It has."

The air stood still as Gina studied her former bully, and that's when she noticed: Kacey Carlisle didn't have any hair. There was only bare skin now, where, in high school, there had been the most incredible, thick auburn hair and the most perfect eyebrows Gina had ever seen. Kacey was bald, and Gina's heart lurched as she considered the most likely reason for the hair loss.

Kacey's eyes were kind when Gina met her gaze.

"How have things been?" she asked.

Gina hesitated, avoiding the question, and Kacey gestured toward the chair, her expression softening into a wistful smile.

"Sit a while. See how you like it."

After glancing at Alex, who gave her the slightest head-tilt to show support, she took Kacey up on the offer.

Kacey gently lowered herself into another nearby chair and set the clipboard in her lap. She faced Gina, her hazel eyes beautiful and unchanged despite what she'd obviously been through.

"Lung cancer," she said. "Came out of nowhere and knocked me clean on my butt. I've never even smoked a single cigarette."

Gina's eyes widened at the abrupt admission. She wasn't sure what she'd expected to come out of Kacey's mouth, but that wasn't it, and a swirl of emotion rose up in her throat.

"Cancer is such an asshole," Gina said tenderly. "I'm so sorry."

"Ain't that the truth," Kacey responded.

The two women talked for a few moments about nothing in particular and within a short while, the unthinkable happened—they were laughing together. Poor Alex, having not moved an inch, glanced between them, looking utterly confused.

When they finally calmed down, Gina pulled herself together and spoke in a serious tone. "Look, Kacey. You and your friends were pretty awful to me growing up, and I don't know if I can forgive you. I wish things were different between us. But I'm sorry you're going through this. You don't deserve it."

Kacey's eyes filled with moisture. "That's...kind of you to say," she said, the words laced with emotion. "Thank you." She paused, a line forming on her forehead as she reached across to put a hand on Gina's knee. "For what it's worth, I am truly sorry I was such a jerk to you."

Gina nodded.

Kacey grinned. "My therapist could tell you lots of reasons why I was such a mean girl back then, but it doesn't matter, does it? In the end, I knew my behavior was wrong and I should have treated you better. If I had it to do over, I would have wanted you to be my friend."

Whether by nature or nurture, Gina was a people pleaser to a fault. But now, she resisted the urge to assuage Kacey's discomfort.

"Thank you for that," she said, knowing it was the best she could give.

"I won't bother you with a catch-up on me or my former friends," Kacey said with a wink. "But I would love to take you for coffee sometime. And what I *will* do is give you half off that tag." She pointed to Gina's chair. "For old times' sake," she added with a nod, her expression revealing much more than her words.

"I'll take it," Gina responded, accepting.

"I'm glad to see you back in town, Gina. I hope you'll take me up on that coffee. I have…things I'd like to say, if you're ever open to it."

Tilting her head slightly, Gina gave a soft smile. She wasn't sure if she would ever take Kacey up on the offer. Some things were meant to stay buried in the past, while others—she glanced at Alex— might be pulled out into the sunshine, dusted off and given a fresh start. Sometimes it was hard to know which was which.

Kacey clapped her hands together and picked up her clipboard as she rose out of her seat.

She turned to Alex. "Do you mind carrying this out for her?"

"Not at all," Alex said, lifting the chair and resting it on his shoulder. "Take care of yourself, Kacey."

"Did you know?" Gina asked when she and Alex had left Kacey's booth. She watched him carefully from the corner of her eye, as he carried the heavy chair overhead as though it weighed nothing.

"No. I had no idea. Not my crowd."

He glanced over at her but she looked away.

"I haven't exactly forgotten how they treated you back then." His voice faltered and turned husky. "They hurt someone I loved…hurt *you*, Gina. Some of my own friends at the time. I told myself they couldn't possibly have meant as much harm as they caused, and I gave them the benefit of the doubt when I shouldn't have. I understand now that I didn't do enough to protect you." He stopped walking and faced her, shifting the big chair so that it didn't cover his brow.

Something pinched inside her at his past tense use of the word *love*, and she had to wonder why. Did she want it to be present tense? Surely not, after everything…

Surely they couldn't go back.

"Regrets like that don't fade easy," he added, his brown eyes searching hers. "Not when it comes to what you and I shared."

But what if they could go forward? What if…

"We were kids, Alex. Kids make mistakes."

Still holding her gaze, he nodded and set down the chair, resting his sun-browned arms against its back.

"Mistakes are a gift, if we let them be…if, after the storm passes and the rubble clears, we look at that mess and see if we can learn from it—if it has anything to teach us."

Lost in the deep rumble of his voice and the darkness in his eyes, Gina forgot about all the years that had passed. Instinct and desire took over and she stepped forward, her body back where it wanted to be, safe in Alex's strong, warm arms.

He didn't say a word as she reached up and pulled his chin toward hers. Heart racing, she blocked out the sights and sounds around her as she closed her eyes and pressed her lips against his.

Back in Sophie's quiet apartment, Gina shut the front door behind her, pressed her back against it and slid to the floor with a heavy sigh.

What in the world had she been thinking, going after Alex like that?

"Oh my God!" Sophie called when she saw Gina—or at least the pile of wobbly mush that resembled her. "Are you okay?"

As Sophie approached and reached for her, Gina opened her eyes and forced her lips into a grim line, far from the unruffled smile she'd been shooting for.

"Yes, I'm fine," she said, pulling herself up off the floor. "Just…having a moment."

Her sister wasn't convinced. "You didn't look fine, slumped on the floor like that. I thought something happened to you." Sophie crossed her arms and leaned against the counter, staring at Gina with obvious skepticism.

Gina shrugged, not yet ready to talk about that kiss with Alex. She hadn't even processed it herself yet. But Sophie was right—something definitely *had* happened to her.

Something had come over her and she'd given in to the irresistible urge to kiss him, against her better judgment. Her emotions were on edge from the heavy encounter with Kacey, the sun had been shining in the perfect blue sky and Alex had been saying things she'd desperately wanted, needed, to hear. All of that bubbled up and overflowed in an incredibly ill-advised move that would only serve to make things far more awkward with him than they had already been.

And that was a pretty high bar.

He was her landlord now, for cripes sake! What had she been thinking?

Sophie's eyes widened when Gina looked up at her.

"Did something happen between you and Alex at the furniture store?"

She gasped before Gina had a chance to answer.

"It did, didn't it?"

Gina bit her bottom lip and looked away, not saying a word, but it didn't matter. Despite their time apart, her sister knew her better than practically anyone.

"Did he kiss you?" Sophie asked, searching Gina's expression, which would probably give everything away.

Breathing in a sigh, Gina pressed a hand to her forehead where the telltale pulse of an impending headache had begun.

"Not exactly," she answered, pushing out the breath.

Sophie frowned. "Well, then what exactly? You're driving me bananas here, sis!"

"I know. I'm sorry. It's just that—"

Just that...what?

And then everything she'd been feeling, everything she'd been holding back, all came flooding out.

"*I* kissed *him*, Soph," she said, watching as her sister's hand flew to her mouth.

"I kissed him because shopping with him turned out to be way more fun than I expected, and he's even more gorgeous now than he was back then, and because when he looked at me with those big brown eyes, I forgot that we weren't together anymore, and I wanted things to be like old times."

"And?" Sophie asked gently, reaching for Gina's hand as she joined her sister on the floor, sitting cross-legged.

Gina closed her eyes and pressed her fingers against her lids, letting the warmth of Sophie's hand on her back serve as a barricade against an onslaught of mixed emotions.

"And because... I've missed him," she admitted, weight coming off of her as the words poured out. "I didn't want to miss him after I left. I tried everything I could to keep it from happening. But I missed him anyway," she said. "Still do, because he's not mine anymore, and he probably won't ever be again."

Sophie squeezed Gina's hand and brushed a

strand of hair from her forehead. "You thought running across the globe would make it easier."

"I did. I really did."

Tears pressed at her lids, but Gina wouldn't let them fall, fearing that if she did they might never cease.

Even though she hadn't wanted to initially, it felt good to open up to her sister.

"I think that's understandable," Sophie said softly. "But you need to figure out what this means and where you're going from here."

Gina shook her head, squeezed Sophie's hand and moved to the refrigerator, where she began pulling things out for dinner.

"It doesn't *mean* anything, and Alex and I aren't *going* anywhere."

She couldn't see her sister, but Gina was pretty sure her statement hadn't been convincing.

"Come on, Gina. You know I know better."

There was an edge to Sophie's voice, part sorrow and part frustration.

Gina plopped a tomato on the cutting board in front of her. She wanted to shout, to release all her anger at Alex. For not trying harder to stop her from going. For not following her when she did. For everything that had happened between them, whether she bore partial responsibility or not. But all she felt then, standing in her sweet sister's kitchen, was heartbroken.

"He's got kids to care for, and the family ranch to run. Both of those require a commitment to this place that I wouldn't be able to offer, even if he wanted me to." She paused, still looking away from her sister. "He's got a life of his own now, Soph," she said, picking up the tomato and passing it back and forth between her hands. "A life that doesn't include me."

She turned to catch Sophie's gaze.

"Is that how you want things to be?"

Though it ached to do so, Gina reached inside and gathered courage, preparing to tell her beloved sister the biggest lie of her life.

"Yes," she breathed, dropping her eyes to the floor. "It's best for everyone if Alex and I keep our distance. So that's how I want it to be."

Chapter Eight

"What was I thinking?" Alex growled. "How in the hell am I supposed to keep my distance from her when she'll be living just a stone's throw away from this house?"

"Language, mijo," his mother chided.

"Ah," Jesse soothed, squeezing his aunt's shoulders, which were at least a foot below his own. "Give him a break, Tia Rosa. He had a rough day yesterday."

Alex glared daggers at his cousin, who'd claimed a soft spot in his mom's heart when they were kids. As the oldest of the bunch, Alex was held to high standards, even as a boy, whereas Jesse could get away with just about anything by flashing that toothpaste-commercial smile of his.

"That is," Jesse continued, "if you consider making out with your gorgeous high school sweetheart a rough time. Seems like there wasn't much *thinking* going on at all."

He winked, and Alex lunged at him, stopping when his mother released an ear-shattering whistle.

"Enough!" she said. "Quit acting like niños and finish helping me with these enchiladas."

Rolling his eyes, he watched as Jesse apologized and kissed Rosa on the cheek, winning her over in an instant. Alex's mother was correct—there was plenty to do before Gina's welcome dinner that night, and little time to do it.

But he'd make sure to pay Jesse back for the ribbing another time.

"I still don't think this is a good idea," Alex said, knowing his words were futile. Once his mom got an idea in her head, there was no stopping her. If she wanted to give Gina a welcome party, she would, and it was best to just say yes to everything and stay out of her way. He supposed he should be thankful Rosa had at least agreed to keep it small—just Alex, her, Jesse and the kids. Gina would likely want to kill him once she arrived and witnessed the modest fanfare, but she probably already did anyway, considering how he'd behaved after that kiss.

Hands busy grating cheese, he looked at the ceiling and released a sigh, remembering the feel of his ex's warm, sweet lips against his. Nothing on earth could have surprised him more than when their eyes met and she reached up to pull him close, taking him back to that place of pure bliss he'd never truly forgotten. In her arms, he'd always found comfort, pleasure…love.

Perhaps that was why he'd pulled away. The reminder of what he'd lost—what he could never have again—hurt too much.

But not as much as the wounded look in her eyes when he'd dazedly brushed the back of his hand across his lips, wiping away the taste of her…

And now she was coming to stay. For who knew how long.

"You okay, my darling?" his mother asked, resting a hand on his forearm until he paused the work and faced her.

Her skin was the same shade of brown as his own, and lined from a life well-lived. It made him think again, as he had so often recently, of the kind of life he craved, the kind of memories he wanted built up when his own hands looked like hers one day.

A partner by his side. Someone to share the burden of running a ranch and raising kids, yes, but also for those little moments that seemed sweeter next to someone you'd chosen for the long haul. Watching the perfect sunset from the back porch. Hearing the kids' squeals of joy when they fed carrots to the horses or opened gifts on Christmas morning.

For so long, those memories he wanted to make had included Gina; it occurred to him that he'd never really been able to picture a future without her. And maybe that explained why dating other people had always felt so forced and stilted, unnatural, like wearing the wrong size boots.

So, why had he rejected her kiss? Why, when she'd reached for him again, perhaps intending to mend what they'd broken, had he turned away?

Because it wasn't real, he reminded himself.

He'd given his heart to Gina before—freely and fully—and she'd shattered it to pieces when she left. He couldn't trust her to protect it then, so why would he trust her now? Whatever the reason for that kiss at the market, it hadn't meant anything, and he needed to put it out of his mind before she took up residence on his land.

"What's on your mind, Alejandro?" his mother said, bringing him back to the present.

"Oh, sorry, Mom." He shook his head to clear the musing. "It's nothing. Just thinking about tomorrow's chores."

The lie sounded pathetic even to him, and she cut through it with a single look.

"I know better than that, my son," Rosa said, patting his arm. "But I also know you're just like your father was. You'll share your thoughts with someone when you're ready." She reached up to squeeze his shoulder, and met his eyes with a warm, knowing gaze. "I just hope it's with the person who most needs to hear them."

Gina stood on the porch of the main house at Trevino Ranch for the second time since she'd come back to Peach Leaf, feeling no less anxious than the first.

The length of her denim shirtdress was perfectly fine, yet she tugged so hard at the hem she worried the stitching might come loose. Only half an hour before, she'd stood in front of Sophie's bathroom mirror, feeling confident despite Alex's rejection the day before. She'd been certain that coming here, going through with moving into the cabin, was the brave thing to do in the face of that terrible moment at the market. She was a grown woman who wasn't going to slink off with her tail between her legs just because some guy didn't want to kiss her back.

Or at least that's how she'd felt back at Sophie's, when her sister proclaimed her dress and red cowboy boots "hot" and her makeup and hair "on point," before every ounce of built-up confidence had run dry.

Now she was more nervous than she'd been meeting her classes on the first day of a new school year.

All because of Alex, who, she was forced to admit, wasn't just *some guy*.

"Bienvenida, my darling!"

The door swung open and Rosa Trevino's warm, rich voice cut through the anxious thoughts going round in her head, and Gina found herself enveloped in a loving embrace, welcomed back into Alex's home like one of the family.

"I can't wait to hear how you've been and get some of my cooking into you! I doubt you've had enchiladas as good as mine in a long time," Rosa said, wrapping Gina into a side hug, her closeness nearly bringing her to tears.

This tiny woman, with her beautiful brown skin and eyes, deceptively strong arms, and a soothing voice that had only ever spoken kind words to her, had basically raised Gina alongside her own sons.

And yet I haven't bothered to call or visit in years.

A wave of regretful sorrow coursed through her as she realized something that should have been obvious before: she hadn't only left Alex and Sophie behind when she'd fled Peach Leaf. Perhaps her absence had wounded Rosa, too, and maybe even the rest of Alex's family.

Perhaps, despite growing up on the wrong side of town—invisible to most people—she mattered more than she had allowed herself to believe.

"Of course I haven't, Tia," she said, her voice shaky with unshed tears. "That would be impossible because no one makes enchiladas like yours."

Rosa squeezed her before letting go. "That's my girl!"

Gina glanced around the kitchen at the beautifully prepared food and the waiting salt-rimmed margarita glasses. From the living room, she could hear Carmen's bubbly giggles, Jesse's laughter and the general raucous sounds of a happy family.

It sounded like home.

"You didn't have to do this, Rosa," Gina said, though her heart filled with the effort they'd put in for her sake.

"Nonsense. We wanted to welcome you back properly, and we didn't think you'd want guests traipsing through your beautiful new space, or a mess to clean up, so we put a little something together here. Nothing excessive. Just you and me, the boys and the grandbabies."

Rosa looked around and threw up her hands. "I just realized you're all alone. ¿Dónde está our Sophie?"

"Oh, she had some inventory to finish at the bookstore. I felt bad leaving her and I know she'll be sorry she missed your cooking."

This was completely untrue—well, at least the part about inventory. Sophie would definitely miss the food. Thinking it would just be Alex giving Gina a tour of the cabin, her sister had refused to come. As if anything was going to happen between them. That ship had obviously sailed…and left a hell of a mess in its wake.

"That's okay. We'll send leftovers," Rosa said. "Now, who wants a drink?"

"I could use one," Alex said, coming in from the living room. He paused when he saw Gina, stuffing his hands into his pockets. "Hey there."

"Hey," she said, swallowing to soothe the dryness in her throat.

Rosa watched the two of them, her expression calm but melancholy, and Gina wondered if she knew about what happened at the outdoor market.

It would be classic Jesse to dig it out of Alex and announce it to the family matriarch.

The Trevino family was tight-knit, and any suggestion that made Gina feel like she belonged in it, though no doubt well-intended, was nothing more than an illusion. She'd given up that possibility long ago, and yesterday's humiliation was a clear reminder.

"Well, let's get those drinks," Rosa said cheerfully.

Moments later they were all settled on the enclosed porch, cocktails in hand. Having greeted her with their opposite, but equally sweet hellos, Eddie and Carmen were occupied by a jigsaw puzzle on a low coffee table in the center of the room, Eddie offering patient help when Carmen deigned to allow it. A trio of ceiling fans circled above, humming the soft sound of a southern summer.

Gina took a sip of her margarita and closed her eyes, relishing the tangy lime, salt and the very best silver tequila. "God, this is good," she said to herself, surprised when the words actually came out of her mouth and everyone laughed.

"Nothing but top-shelf in this house," Rosa said. "This is what Alex's dad and I made to celebrate when we first moved in," she added, her smile fading a little. "I was so intimidated by the idea of being a ranch wife."

Gina watched Alex and Jesse roll their eyes at each other. They'd all heard this story many times. For Gina, it never got old, and she knew, in spite of their behavior, that the guys felt the same. There was comfort in their family history. In knowing that, though the world changed constantly around them, the ranch, their home, could always be counted on to stand steady.

Though she'd never wanted to admit such a thing, especially to Alex, there was undeniable appeal in the idea.

Gina took another sip, willing the alcohol to smooth the sharp edges of a familiar ache that swept in when she'd set foot inside this house, her body seeming to reabsorb the memories within its walls.

"What did I know about ranching," Rosa continued. "Me? A city girl from Houston. Ha!" She set her glass down to better gesture with her hands, each finger adorned by at least one ring. "That first week of marriage was so hard I nearly said adios to Eduardo and hightailed it back to my studio apartment." She took a deep breath. "I missed my friends something awful, and the nights were so dark and quiet out here, I thought I'd die if I didn't see the city lights again."

"But you survived, Tia, didn't you?" Jesse chimed in, winking at Gina. "You lived to tell the tale."

"And tell it she does," Alex added with a grin. "As often as she can, to anyone who will listen."

Rosa reached over to swat her son, and Gina couldn't help herself. A laugh came out so hard she nearly choked on her margarita, eyes stinging as the liquor seared her throat.

"You okay there?" Alex asked, around a barely suppressed chuckle.

She nodded. "No big deal. Don't look too sorry for me, now," she teased.

Or I might get the idea that you care.

"Oh, I feel sorry, all right," he said, brown eyes twinkling with mischief. "Sorry I didn't get it on camera."

Gina opened her mouth wide, feigning shock.

"You'd better watch it, coz," Jesse said. "Gina can kick your ass from here to Sunday, and we all know it. At least according to Sophie."

"What?" Gina asked.

"Oh, she told me you started taking Krav Maga years ago, when you got your first teaching assignment and were going to travel overseas on your own. Smart," he said, nodding in obvious admiration.

This time, the shock in her expression was real.

"I can't believe she told you that." The barest inkling of a question bubbled up around the edges of her consciousness. "When did you last talk to Sophie?"

Jesse's high-boned cheeks turned a remarkable shade of red, the likes of which Gina had never seen on the chronic playboy bachelor's face.

"Good question," Alex added, staring at his cousin with a single raised brow. Rosa's gaze, too, was fixed on her nephew.

Instead of relishing the undivided attention of several people the way he usually would, Jesse appeared to clam up.

"Oh, uh, you know. It was the… I went into the bookstore the other day to pick up something to read."

"Now I *know* you're full of it," Alex said.

Gina watched in awe as the pieces clicked together. Sophie's refusal to come with her wasn't just to give Gina and Alex time alone—she had guessed that her sister would pick up on anything going on between her and Jesse. Add to that Sophie's avoidance when Gina asked if she was dating anyone new. Of the two sisters, Sophie had always been more outgoing, which made her a heck of a saleswoman, and an excellent hostess. But she'd stuck mostly to the shop since Gina had been home.

Were Jesse and Sophie *together*? Or did Sophie just have a crush on him?

It was an astonishing development, and Gina would definitely do some digging the next day when she and Sophie planned to move most of her stuff into the cabin. But in the meantime she could see Jesse struggling, and she wanted to help him out of his misery.

"He's legit," Gina said, earning surprised expressions from everyone in the room. "I saw him there the other day, buying a gift."

"Uncle Jesse doesn't like to read!" Carmen shouted, grinning from ear to ear when her outburst earned a bout of laughter from the adults.

"He does sometimes, Carmen. He reads us stories when he comes to visit," Eddie said. Jesse reached over to scrub his nephew's mop of hair.

"Yeah," Jesse said, his voice cracking a little. "I was buying a gift, which is none of your business, coz." Confidence renewed, he puffed out his chest and took a sip of his margarita. "Now, if I remember correctly, Tia was telling her favorite story."

Rosa's features displayed obvious conflict between wanting to hear more about this possible… thing…between her favorite nephew and her darling Sophie, and finishing her beloved narrative, but she clasped her hands together and charged ahead.

"So, as I was saying, I thought I would just shrivel up and die out here in the country and float away on the wind like a tumbleweed."

At this, Carmen abandoned the puzzle, curled herself into a ball and proceeded to somersault across the floor in her best tumbleweed demonstration. Everyone, including a very gracious Eddie, applauded.

"Gracias for the wonderful visual effects, Carmenita. Now, where was I?" Rosa tucked a finger against her chin and then pointed it in the air. "Oh yes! I thought I was going to wilt out here in the middle of nowhere. But then I remembered my mother saying that the first year of marriage is the hardest, and that I needed friends to get me through it. So I went into town, marched straight into the coffee shop, which, of course—" she pointed around the room at each of them "—was not a coffee shop but a soda fountain at the time, and who did I find but my favorite girls!"

"Estelle, Sandy, Quita and Janine," chimed Alex and Jesse in sync.

Rosa's eyes sparkled as she relived the past, her audience entranced despite having heard this a million times before.

"They were all there for the same reason! All of us from different cities, newly married to those country boys, not one of us with a clue as to what we were doing."

Carmen climbed into Jesse's lap and Eddie nodded to a silent rhythm of his own, reabsorbed in the puzzle.

"We talked for hours, our husbands all at home wondering what on earth happened to us, and every week since then, we've met at that same spot."

Jesse didn't miss his cue. Smiling warmly at his aunt, he asked, "And what do you ladies do there, Tia?"

Rosa's cheeks filled with the color of her namesake. "Well, we exchange recipes and advice, and we talk about everything under the sun. From how to manage knuckleheaded niños, to how to keep our husbands from driving us crazy, when they were all here with us, of course, and we prop each other up during hard times."

Her eyes met Gina's, and Gina had to look away to keep emotion from welling up.

"There have been quite a few of those," Rosa said.

Gina felt the older woman's gaze on her.

"But you have to keep going anyway. And you have to let the people who love you help you stay standing."

"Just like Eddie helps me up when I run too fast and fall down!" Carmen shouted, to a chorus of affectionate approval.

"Just like that, sweetie," Alex agreed.

When Gina looked up, his eyes met hers and she began sinking into them, their depths impossible to resist.

And yet she did resist, pulling her gaze away because she had to. Because she had put herself out there, taken a chance on a simple kiss just to test the water. She hadn't asked him to forget their shared past or the pain harbored within. Only a little kiss—a gesture to suggest that maybe, just maybe, she would be willing to try again, if he was.

Well, he'd given his answer. Whether she liked it or not, she had to try to accept it. Things were over between them, and that's how it would remain.

So why was he looking at her like that? Irritation boiled inside her. If he *didn't want* her, why couldn't he stop looking at her that way, like a drooping wildflower lifting its face to the promise of long-awaited rain?

Without a word, Gina grabbed her glass and left

the porch, heading for the kitchen. Fuming as she bent over the big porcelain farm sink, she washed the goblet clean, lifting her wrists to let the cool water run over her veins and calm her racing pulse.

After a few seconds passed, she felt a presence behind her and shut the water off, setting the glass in the drying rack before pulling free a towel to wipe her hands.

"What do you want, Alex?" she asked without turning. "Because we both know it isn't me."

"It's only me, precious girl," Rosa said softly.

Gina spun around, cheeks burning with embarrassment.

"Oh, Rosa, I…"

She stepped closer and tugged the towel from Gina's death grip before guiding her to the kitchen table.

"Come with me, dear. Let's sit for a moment."

As they took their chairs, Gina was suddenly exhausted. "I am so thankful you invited me here today, and I'm beyond grateful that you agreed Alex could let me stay on the ranch—and don't argue because I know he wouldn't have done it without your blessing—so, I don't mean to be rude, but I don't think I have the energy to talk much today, Tia. It's been a strange week, and I'm just trying to figure out what to do about a lot of things, and…"

"It's okay," Rosa said, wearing a soft, understanding smile. "How about *I* talk, and you just sit and let me share a few things? How does that sound?"

Gina nodded hesitantly.

Rosa's warm brown eyes, so similar to her son's, soothed Gina's nerves. A sense of being in the exact right place at the right time flooded through her, overwhelming and powerful, filling so many empty spaces in Gina's heart.

"First," Rosa said, taking Gina's hand, "I just want to tell you that we've missed you. Alex, Jesse and I."

"I've missed you, too," Gina said, the words rushing out. "I'm so sorry I haven't visited. It's not that I didn't want to, it's just—"

Rosa shook her head. "You don't owe me an explanation," she said, moving her hand from Gina's to wave it gently. "We all have to make choices the best we know how, with what we have at any given moment. I was very, very grateful to have you in our lives when you were young. I cherished every moment. Did I hope that would continue?" She paused, giving a wink and a grin. "Of course

I did. You made Alex happy…happier than anyone ever has."

While this admission did nothing to change Gina's feelings about his rejection of the kiss she'd offered, it did quell her anger and frustration at seeing him today, and those mixed messages he seemed to be sending. A little, anyhow.

"But I know you had to spread your wings and see what lay beyond this little town." Rosa closed her eyes and breathed deeply before opening them. "I imagine it can be suffocating, at times, to grow up in a place like this. Small towns aren't always friendly to everyone. I was lucky to find my place, my people here, early on, and that made it easier for me, but it's not always that way."

"Don't I know it," Gina whispered.

"Especially," Rosa continued, nodding in agreement, "when the people responsible for helping you grow and figure out who you are, aren't up for the job."

A tickle started at the back of her throat, along with the sudden pressure of tears behind her eyes. To keep them from falling, Gina turned her attention to the surrounding kitchen. Updated but familiar, it still retained the coziness she'd always cherished. Over the sink, a window faced onto the front porch and she could see the rocker and swing that had always been there, repainted a deep azure over the strong, sharp-scented cedar Mr. Trevino had cut and crafted it from.

"I went by the old apartment complex yesterday," Gina said, her voice shaking. "It was so run-down. I've taught all over the world, and I know it's much worse for a lot of kids, and Sophie and I didn't starve or anything—"

"Though there were a few times," Rosa interrupted gently, "when it got a little close, didn't it?"

Gina nodded, eyes focused on the navy blue roller shade above the window. "Sophie usually tried to save a little something from her lunch at school for us," Gina said. "And of course there were the amazing meals at your house."

She hoped the compliment would urge Rosa to change the subject. It had always been more than a little difficult to talk about her parents, and their lack of, well, whatever it was that made other parents better at their jobs. But Rosa stayed the course.

"I always wanted to speak about this when you and your sister were growing up, but the time never seemed quite right." She rubbed her fingers across the many, jeweled rings on her free hand. "Or maybe I should have anyway and didn't because

I was afraid I might hurt you. Now, I'm afraid I may have done you harm by *not* speaking about it."

"It's okay," Gina soothed. "You took care of us more than anyone else, and I wish I'd taken the time to thank you earlier. Before I…before I left town."

"I didn't need to hear the words to know that," Rosa said, meeting Gina's gaze. "And I wish I had done more. But I've had a lot of time, since losing my husband and my oldest son, to think about what it means to be a parent, where I feel I succeeded and where I could have done better with my own children."

Rosa stopped fidgeting and folded her hands in her lap before speaking again.

"Your father had his own demons to contend with after your mother left him and you girls." She reached out again, covering Gina's hand with her own. "I'm not excusing his behavior, dear. Plenty of single parents grieve their losses and manage to pull themselves together and do what they need to for the kids they brought into the world. But for reasons I don't understand, that is not the path your dad took, and I know his choices hurt you and Sophie. I just want you to understand that it wasn't, and isn't, your fault. Not his behavior, or your mother's abandonment. Not any of it."

The excessive drinking, the absence, the neglect…

Gina nodded, tears brimming now. She knew it wasn't her fault that her mother left when she and Sophie were small, or that her father wasn't much of one, long before Mrs. Trevino said the words out loud. But on some level, underneath the logic, the reasons, and the therapy, didn't every neglected child wonder, just as Gina always had—*if I had been better in some way, more lovable somehow, would my parents have still given up on me?*

It was a question she would probably always carry, a burden she'd done her best to accept. But being with Alex again for just a short time, allowing herself to daydream a future with him, even if it wasn't based in reality…a future with him and those sweet, funny, smart kids…made her want to try harder to let go of that burden.

Somehow, she knew letting go was the key to becoming whole. Because how could she ask Alex to love her again, if she didn't believe herself worthy of being loved at all?

Chapter Nine

"Thank you," she said through tears. "It means a lot to hear you say that."

Rosa nodded before pulling Gina into a firm embrace. "I know it would be better coming from your own folks, but I've always been happy to stand in for them, and I hope I've done a good job."

"The best," Gina said softly before pulling back to meet Rosa's eyes. "You've done the best job. And it is so wonderful to get to see you again."

"Well, you'll be seeing a great deal of me. Don't think for a minute that I won't come down to that cabin and check on you if you try to act like a stranger again," Rosa warned.

"As long as you bring me something to eat, you

can check on me anytime you like," Gina retorted, making them both giggle.

"What's going on?" Alex asked, poking his head into the kitchen.

Gina and Rosa continued laughing together, even as the few tears remaining from their heart-to-heart ran down their cheeks.

"None of your business, mijo," Rosa answered, waving him away. She turned back to Gina. "I'd better go check on the other kids. All three of them," she said with a wink. "And I know you're probably anxious to see your new place."

"Thank you," Gina said, "for everything."

Rosa nodded, gently squeezing Alex's arm before heading back in the direction of the porch, where Gina could hear Jesse making animal noises and the kids' ensuing laughter.

"What bad things did she tell you about me?" Alex asked with a grin. "I promise none of it's true."

"I'm not so sure about that," Gina said, more seriously than she intended.

"Hey," he said. "What's wrong?"

"*What's wrong?* Are you joking, Alex?"

Her eyes burned into his. Could he really not see how mad she was? How hurt?

"Alex, I don't know if you remember this," she

said, her tone laced with bitter sarcasm, "but I tried to kiss you yesterday, and you completely blew me off."

At least he had the decency to look ashamed.

"About that," he said. "Gina, I'm sorry. I was surprised, is all, and I didn't know how to react."

She folded her arms protectively across her chest.

"Well, the usual way to react to someone kissing you is to kiss them back, unless you're repulsed by them. Then you react…pretty much the way you did," she said, fuming more and more by the second. "I put myself out there, Alex, and you made me feel like a complete and total fool."

"You put yourself out there? *You?* What about what I did, Gina? I offered you a home, for God's sake. After you—" He sucked in a breath. "You know what, never mind." He glanced at the kitchen doorway. "I'm not doing this now."

"Good! I don't want to do this, whatever *this* is, now, or ever," Gina said, careful not to raise her voice too much. As frustrated as she was, his glance at the entrance told her he didn't want everyone to hear, especially the kids. And she didn't either. There had been enough fighting in her own home growing up, before her mother left, and enough heartbreaking conversations between her and Alex, as well, before *Gina had* left town.

In the pause, Alex's expression had softened, and he was looking at her as though he wanted to say something, despite having just made it very clear that he didn't.

"Look, Gina," he said gently. "That's not what I meant. We do have things to talk about, you and I. I just think it needs to be done in private. Just the two of us. There are things I need you to hear."

Pulse thudding in her ears, she stared at him, wanting, but struggling, to stay mad.

"Come on, I'll show you the cabin. Jesse can help my mom clean up here, and they can put a movie on and hang out with the kids. I know we have our issues, but I still want you... I want you to stay."

The words felt so familiar.

The whole damn thing felt so familiar.

Him standing there, asking her to stay, knowing full well all she really wanted was to get as far away from him as possible. It begged the question: Why the hell did he keep putting himself in this situation? Why did he keep asking her to stay in one place long enough to sort out what went wrong between them? To make the effort. To choose him. When it was clear she never would.

And yet there was that kiss.

Intentions be damned, it had given him hope he didn't want. And here he was, again, letting that hope pull him along like a dog on a leash.

"Fine," she said. "Some of my things are in the car. If you want, I can get them and meet you down there."

Hell if he was going to let her tell him what to do.

"I'll ride with you," he declared, and Gina had the nerve to grin. He couldn't really blame her; even he had to admit it was a pretty pathetic attempt to regain control.

Silently, they walked out to her car, an older model Hyundai that had seen better days. Gina had never been interested in material things, or buying the latest rendition of something just because it was new when an older version still worked perfectly well. It was one of many things he liked about her.

The sun was setting over the horizon, washing the ranchland in soft shades of tangerine and purple. Dusk would soon fall around them. It was his favorite time of day, when the work was finished and he had the evening to spend with Carmen and

Eddie. Sometimes his mom and Jesse too. It felt natural, today, having Gina back among them. Almost as if she'd been there all along.

The thought softened his mood a little as she drove down the gravel path toward the cabin, her eyes trained straight ahead, the only sound that of pebbles crunching under her car tires.

When they reached the cabin, Alex got out and went to Gina's door. He opened it for her and reached for her hand. For a second, he thought she might shove it aside. And if she had, he would have helped her bring her overnight stuff inside, made sure she had what she needed for the night and the next morning, and left it at that. He could imagine things playing out that way, and he would have forced himself to accept it if they had.

But rarely did life present only one path, and this was no different.

So when Gina folded her hand in his, her warm fingers curling into his palm, she surprised him for the second time in as many days. And he should have expected as much from the woman who'd captured his heart all those years ago. This intrepid, tenacious, stubborn, beautiful, brave woman.

Emotion welled up; instead of meeting her eyes, he looked at their hands, woven together again as if they'd never separated. A wave of nostalgia threatened to overwhelm him as Alex pictured all the years they could have spent together instead of being apart.

But along with that nostalgia and regret came a new understanding.

Maybe it wasn't all about him.

Maybe leaving town was Gina's way of managing past pain. Maybe it was a gift she'd allowed herself, of peace and space and time to heal. From the way she'd been treated by kids at school. From the heartbreak of her mother walking out when she and Sophie were still so small. From her father's neglect.

From Alex's own inability to offer her a life filled with adventure and new experiences, at least at that time.

But as the regret cleared, it left room for something else, something better: possibility. He glimpsed the beginnings of a way forward, and for a moment, he didn't turn away.

Maybe if she stayed, if they gave each other another chance, they could work through some of the problems they'd ignored. And if they could find a way back to each other, when the kids were a little bit older, maybe they could have adventures together.

As a family.

Maybe they didn't even have to wait until the kids were older.

Suddenly, he found himself hoping against all odds that she would ignore his damn foolishness the day before and try to kiss him again…

"Alex?"

He shook his head and stared at her as he pulled himself back down into the real world, where most people weren't lucky enough to get a second chance.

"Yeah?"

Gina cocked her head, and one corner of her mouth ticked up as she cast a pointed look at their joined hands. "Are you going to help me out so we can unload the car?"

"Yeah, yeah!" he said, far too eager.

He assisted her out of the vehicle and let go of her hand, the warmth of her skin lingering when their flesh no longer touched.

He stepped backward and Gina moved to the trunk of the car. Inside were only a couple of duffel bags; Alex slung one over each shoulder and walked up the steps while Gina followed slowly behind.

"These are gorgeous," she called, pointing to the raised cedar beds Jesse had built around the base of the porch.

"They will be in the spring, anyway," Alex said,

digging a key out of his pocket. "When you plant something in them." Unspoken words tugged at his heart: *If you're still here.*

"I'll ask your mom to help me," she said lightly. "I'm a bit of a serial killer when it comes to plants."

Key in hand, he watched her walk up the steps.

"Anything green is pretty much DOA with me." She paused. "Of course, maybe that will change if I'm not traveling so often."

Their eyes met and neither said a word for a long moment.

Could other things change too? he wondered.

Alex realized he'd been holding the key with a death grip so tight it left dents in his palm when he placed it into the lock. The door squeaked a little when it opened, and he made a mental note to fix it later.

Still shouldering the bags, he held out an arm to usher her in. "All yours."

Gina raised an eyebrow and looked him up and down in a way that heated his blood.

"Aren't you going to carry me over the threshold?" she asked, her tone undeniably flirty.

He swallowed, frozen in place, nearly dropping the bags.

"I'm just kidding, Alex," she said, clearly enjoying his discomfort. "Goodness. Calm down."

"I knew that," he said.

Good one.

God, what the hell was wrong with him?

Grinning, she walked past him into the little house. He caught a heady mix of lavender and vanilla as she did, and he admired the sway of her body in the sexy dress she wore, a long denim shirtdress, cinched where her waist curved inward. He made himself look away when his eyes slid down to those red cowgirl boots, as thoughts filled his head of slipping them off one at a time, tossing them onto the floor...

He was out of practice, that was all. Since adopting the kids, he hadn't made any time for dating. His mom offered to take them when he needed a break, but he'd wanted to give them consistency, stability, a predictable routine they could rely on day-to-day to create some semblance of a "normal" life. As much as one could after losing their mom and dad so young.

Truth be told, he hadn't been in the mood for dating. Grief settled in after his brother and sister-in-law died, and Carmen and Eddie had been the only balm. Even on the darkest days when his home was filled with their tears, their warm little arms around him made things bearable until enough time had passed that he could go out into the world. Together, somehow, their little trio had reached functionality again, and the risk of bringing someone else into the mix, the possible disruption it could cause, was too high.

Until Gina arrived and fit right in.

The kids liked her. His mom and Jesse adored her.

And Alex loved her still, for God's sake.

And even though that kiss, however brief, had slid under his skin and threatened to undo him, he couldn't trust her to stick around. If he let her into their lives, stood by while Eddie and Carmen grew to rely on her presence, and she got a wild hair again or got scared of commitment, what then? They'd been through enough heartbreak already, had sure as hell suffered enough loss. He couldn't, in good conscience, put them through that again or they might not make it out okay this time.

Neither would he.

But there she was, gorgeous as a summer sky as she wandered around the cabin, admiring all the little touches his cousin had put in just for her. Because they all wanted her to stay, to choose them.

The damn lot of them were spellbound.

And he was no exception.

She caught his gaze, then glanced downward, suddenly shy. "Do you want to come in? If I know your mom, there's soda in the fridge, and probably beer."

At his hesitation, she added, "Look, I'm just being polite. You don't have to stay long, or you could just say no."

How misguided she was, if she thought he could turn down the chance to spend another moment with her.

"Sure," he said, stepping into the barely there foyer. "Where would you like me to put these?"

"Um…" She did a little spin, then bit her bottom lip as her cheeks flooded with obvious heat. "In the bedroom if you don't mind."

Meeting her eyes, he nodded. And thank the stars she didn't follow him because he needed the time to cool off before heading back toward the kitchen.

He found her there, rustling around in the fridge. "I can give you a tour, if you like."

"That would be great," she said. "Ah. A six-pack and a nice bottle of white. Just as I suspected."

He had to laugh. "And if you open that cabinet to the right, you'll find a set of stemless wineglasses and a pair of mugs. Mom's not to be bested as a hostess."

"Never," she agreed, eyes sparkling at the humor.

"But I'm good after the margarita. It's been a while since I've had anything that strong."

"Same," Alex said. "I don't drink around the kids, and if I ever did it would be a single beer, not Mom and Dad's ass-kicking margaritas."

Gina tilted her head back and laughed. "Those suckers will put hair on your chest, won't they?"

"They're legendary around town. All the Uber drivers know they'll have a good haul when Mom throws a party," Alex said, nodding.

"For Cinco de Mayo, the Fourth, Thanksgiving, Halloween, Christmas…"

"St. Patrick's Day, Boxing Day, Grandparents' Day…" he added.

"Opposite Day, Pi Day…"

"National Peanut Butter and Jelly Day…"

The list got more and more ridiculous, and by the time they'd listed enough absurd holidays to fill a calendar, they were both laughing uncontrollably.

"So," Gina said, wiping at her eyes. "Water?"

"Sure."

She pulled out two glasses and filled them from a filter pitcher in the fridge. His mom had outdone herself in her obvious ploy to secure a daughter-in-law, and he would make sure to bug her about it later.

Gina lifted herself up to perch on a corner of the countertop while Alex stood, eyes focused on the water to better ignore the sight of her bare legs in those red boots.

She glanced around the cabin, and he followed her gaze. Tiny though it was, Jesse had done good work. The living area boasted high ceilings, a window with a stunning view of the creek that ran through the property, and a built-in bookcase and desk with a chair. Alex insisted his cousin leave it bare, so that Gina could choose her own fabric and do the upholstery herself. If she liked the idea and was happy with the outcome, he'd suggest taking photos of the project for a small ad. He knew a guy at the local paper who would run it for him if he asked.

As much as he might try, he couldn't seem to stop himself from thinking ahead, planning for the future.

"It really is awesome," she said, seeming to read his thoughts. "I can't wait for Sophie to see it."

He smiled. "Do you have much stuff to move in tomorrow? I'd be glad to bring my truck and help if you need it."

Gina's lips formed a straight line. "Sadly, no," she said, taking a sip of her water as she looked out across the living room. "Casualty of a nomadic life, I'm afraid. I'm so thankful you guys had extra furniture."

The mention of furniture brought to mind the chair from their market trip, and the…incident that happened. A glance at Gina's closed-off expression confirmed she'd followed the same line of thinking.

"Plus you've got the chair," he said. Maybe facing the thing straight on was the best approach.

"About that," Gina began, before pausing to stare into her water glass. "I shouldn't have done it. Tried to kiss you." She looked up and met his eyes. "It was a happy moment after one of the better days I've had in a while, and it felt good spending time with you again, and I guess I just got a little carried away."

He took a deep breath. "You regret it, don't you?" he asked, his tone revealing too much hope.

"I didn't say that."

They were quiet for several seconds.

"Do you?" he urged.

"Short answer? No."

"Is there a longer version?" he asked, unable to keep the desperation out of his voice.

Still holding his gaze, she set down the glass.

"It's *you*, Alex. I think you know this. I don't think I have to say it out loud, but when it comes to *you*, there's a part of me that could never regret a kiss, or anything else."

Alex swallowed, feeling the rise and fall of his chest as his breathing sped up.

"But?"

"But that doesn't mean things aren't still complicated between us. There's a reason you stopped that kiss, isn't there? It's the same reason that a little part of me *does* regret it. I think we both know we can't go back to the way things were. We can't reclaim the past and undo the fact that you asked me to stay, and I said no. I think that even if I had changed my mind and stayed…a part of you would always resent me for that."

He clung to one piece of what she'd said. "Have you?"

"What?" she asked.

"Changed your mind. Have you changed your mind about what happened? You could have chosen a college nearby—we both know that. But if you had it to do over again, would you still have left when I asked you to stay with me, to live with me, to choose me over…whatever it was you were looking for out there?"

"Alex—"

"I need to know, Gina. I need to hear this."

"Why, Alex? What good is it going to do?"

He could hear the budding frustration in her voice, the fatigue that always seemed to accompany rehashing old disagreements, old hurts.

"I know it's selfish of me to ask, and I know you needed more than this town had to offer, but I want to know why you were willing to take a chance on an unknown future, on setting out alone with no net beneath you, but you weren't willing to take a chance on me."

His heart raced from the effort of telling the truth, but also with relief from having said what he'd needed to all these years.

Her knuckles were pale where they gripped the countertop, and her eyes pleaded with him to release her from having this conversation.

Lifting a hand, she pressed fingers into her forehead.

"Alex, it's always been easy for you to imagine a life with me. The two of us getting married, maybe raising a family, growing old together and being happy. But that's because you had those things in front of you to set an example. They were reality for you because you saw them every day in your mom and dad. But for me…for me, those things were nothing but a fantasy. It was possible for you to take risks for love, because you've always had a supportive family behind you, to catch you if you fall, and even the ranch to ground you. I had none of those things, Alex."

He pulled in a breath.

"I hear what you're saying, Gina. But once upon a time, I offered to share those things with you. I wanted more than anything to share those things with you. My family, my home…all of it. And you turned me down."

She shook her head, obviously frustrated that they didn't see eye to eye.

"And if I'd taken that risk with you? If I'd committed and stayed and married you, and it hadn't worked out, what would I have done? Where would I have gone?" Her arms flung out to her sides. "This town has always embraced you, Alex. It wasn't the same for me. If you and I had failed, *I* would have been expected to leave. Not you."

There was some truth to that, he had to admit. But it wasn't that simple.

"So you just pulled the plug and decided our fate for the both of us, without even trying. You couldn't have stuck around, waited for me to sort things out after my dad passed? I don't know if I would have been able to follow you, but at least we could have figured out the future together. We could have tried to find a way…*together*. It wasn't a picnic, Gina, taking over this place at that age. I had a lot to learn, and it would have been a hell of a lot better if I'd had you by my side."

Her eyes fell and a few tears slipped down her cheeks. With shaking hands, she wiped them away.

He wanted so badly to hold her, to soften the emotional blow he'd dealt. But he needed her to understand his side of things, if there was any hope of their moving forward together.

"You were worth it, Alex. You still are. I just couldn't deal with the thought of things not working out between us. I wouldn't have just lost you, Alex, which would have been terrible enough. I would have lost my family as well. Not my father, but the only family I really had besides Sophie—yours. The cost was too high, and I was too afraid of what might happen if we failed to stay together."

He stepped closer.

"But you didn't *lose* us, Gina. You *left* us. We're still here," he said, moving even closer.

He drew near enough that her knees brushed his torso, and he set his glass down next to hers on the counter.

"*I'm* still here."

Chapter Ten

Gina's breath hitched in her throat as Alex's chest grazed her knees. His eyes, dark and full of longing, held questions she wasn't sure she was ready to answer. Reaching forward, she pressed a hand into that wall of warm muscle.

"What is this, Alex?" she asked, her words unsteady as her thoughts began to spin. "Yesterday, you didn't even want to kiss me. You made that clear. So what are you saying? What's changed?"

"I'm saying I made a mistake. I shouldn't have pushed you away like that. If you're here, truly here, and you want to try again, try *us* again, I'm willing to make that leap with you."

Was he offering what she thought he was? Another chance? And if so, should she take it? Did she even want it?

Despite all the time that had passed, she knew she needed more to be certain. Perhaps things were a bit clearer, now that she was sure her attraction, her feelings for him, hadn't faded—had in fact grown stronger—but she still wasn't sure she could promise what he wanted.

A life together. Forever.

She still had work to do, on herself, *for* herself. And she owed it to him to be honest about that.

"I'm not positive about what I want, Alex. And I can't make any promises until I figure that out."

She prepared herself for his reaction, anticipating the worst.

He nodded, slowly, brow creasing as he seemed to consider her words. But he didn't pull back like she thought he might. Instead, he moved closer until she could feel the gentle breeze of his breath on her neck, see the growing hunger in his eyes.

He reached up and curved his hand against her temple, running his fingers along her jawline until they reached her chin. Cupping it, he pulled her toward him.

"I realize I'm going to have to live with that for now, Gina. Because I *do* know what I want. I've always known."

He moved forward until their lips touched softly. Closing his eyes, he held the gentle kiss until she folded into him. He pressed lightly with his tongue and she opened her mouth, leaning in closer, deepening the pressure as his hands moved to her waist.

Heart pounding into her ribs, the nerves along her spine awakening at his touch, Gina spread her knees apart. Alex responded by running his hands along the tops of her thighs, lighting a trail of electricity that only intensified when it reached her waist. With only the thin cotton of her underwear between his hands and her flesh, he cupped her bottom and lifted her against him, carrying her across the kitchen and into the living room.

When they reached the couch, he lay her back against the soft cushions, keeping his palm behind her head until it rested against a pillow. Holding her gaze, he pressed one knee into the couch to brace himself as he lifted her legs one at a time to pull off her boots. When her feet were bare, he held one in his palm, pressing kisses up the length of her calf before sliding his hand along behind.

Her breathing came in short spurts and her palms began to sweat as her pulse went haywire. Gina couldn't recall when she'd last experienced such desire, such desperation for release, and the seriousness in Alex's expression, his darkened eyes when he looked up at her, told her his hunger matched her own.

She'd imagined this exact situation a number of times, remembering what it was like to be full of someone she'd loved, especially on occasions when intimacy with others had disappointed her. With Alex, it had always been easy and delicious, and she'd imagined it would be the same should they ever find their way back to one another. Yet until today, she'd stopped believing such a thing could happen.

But there he was, and the fire in his touch revealed how much he wanted to be. As he'd said, maybe that was enough. Maybe for now, she could live with just knowing his body again. Maybe she didn't need to win his heart as well.

And much to her amazement, being with him again wasn't the same at all. Not even close. Whatever the reasons—maturity, experience, intensified fondness born of long separation—this was different. Better. More urgent. She ached for them to come together.

"I want this, Gina, more than anything," he said, lifting her dress as he lay a path of kisses along her belly. "Do you?"

Unable to form sound, she nodded.

"I need to hear you say it. Please." He lifted his

mouth and instantly she missed the hot press of his lips against her skin.

"Yes," she said, biting her lower lip. "I want this. I want you."

A lock of ebony hair fell over his brow as he grinned, eyes hooded with the anticipation of pleasure.

He was beautiful, even more so with age, she thought, entranced as she watched him draw closer until he hovered over her, his arms caging her. Bending down, he covered her mouth and she groaned as his tongue explored, finding hers.

She pulled away, near breathless from his kiss.

"Alex," she began. "I hate to interrupt, but we need to talk about protection. I'm on the pill, but… are you safe?"

He pushed up, making space between them. "Of course," he said. "Yes. I'm safe. I've been tested and I have something on me." He paused to retrieve his wallet from a pocket of his jeans, pulling out a condom. "I just want you to know it's been a long time, Gina. A very long time."

Closing her eyes, she nodded, then pulled in a deep breath.

He stared at her as though worried she might change her mind, yet she knew with complete confidence that if she did, he wouldn't hesitate to slam on the brakes.

"Say the word and we'll stop."

"I don't want to stop," she said.

With that, his lips quirked up in a smile that still held the power to dismantle her staunchest defenses, and her stubborn heart unfolded. Alex undid his jeans and shoved them off, leaning over her again. He traced a finger along the inside of her thigh and it trailed under her panties, where he brought her to the brink, teasing and coaxing until she let go. Then she reached forward and, feeling the warm weight of him in her hand, led him to her center. He filled her as they moved in harmony, riding a wave of pleasure she hoped wouldn't end, and they held on to each other as though in a silent promise to never let go again.

A few mornings later, Alex woke before dawn and immediately reached toward the other side of the bed, fingers itching to caress Gina though of course she wasn't there.

He was in his own room at the main house, and if he knew Gina, she would still be sleeping in her new bed at the cabin, tucked in between the satiny sheets she'd brought—sheets he'd gotten to know quite well over the past week.

Rolling out of bed, he dressed, grabbed a thermos of coffee and went about his chores as the sun began to rise, laughing here and there with fresh amazement as both his mind and body recalled the moments they'd been stealing together every chance they could.

Gina's soft, smooth skin under his fingertips. Her mouth hot and wet against his lips and later, against the rest of him. Her eyes sparkling with lust as sharp as his own as she pulled him toward her, longing to have him inside her as much as he ached to feel her warm flesh around him, again and again.

Being with her had never been short of amazing, but this was different, special, as if they both needed to make up for lost time.

With that thought, Alex glanced at his watch. They had a big day ahead, and he needed to get a move on. He and Gina, his mom and the kids, were meeting Vanessa and her family at the wildflower center, where they would walk the trails and have a picnic lunch together. He couldn't wait to spend time with his favorite people in the world, but he'd be lying to himself if he didn't admit there was some apprehension in the mix as well.

Sure, she had gotten along well with Van when they'd met at his friend's shop. But spending several hours together was a different situation, and it was important to him that his closest friends got along with his…well, what was she?

He'd meant what he said when he told her he was okay with uncertainty for the time being, and he knew she wasn't ready to offer what he wanted—permanence, commitment, her heart. But there were moments when he thought she might be close, moments when he thought they might be getting somewhere. She seemed to love her cabin, and it brought him joy to see her making the space her own, choosing fabric for chairs and curtains and filling it with her creations. She'd even started a few commission projects for folks around town, thanks to the reach of his mom's squad.

But he got the feeling she'd do the same if she were starting a new teaching gig in Taiwan, or Panama, or Belize. As a person who moved a lot, he imagined she knew how to make a temporary home anywhere. He knew he would have to ask her how she felt soon, whether she'd given any further thought to staying in Peach Leaf, but he was hesitant to press her, worried it would cause her to put up her defenses and they'd lose the good thing they had going.

The questions gnawed at him as he finished checking fences on the north side of the ranch, and continued through the morning as he rousted Eddie out of bed (hard; took three or four tries) and Carmen (easy; took less than one). He fed the kids scrambled eggs, and toast with Van's home-made strawberry jam, then took his laptop into the living room to catch up on bookkeeping while the kids watched Saturday morning cartoons.

He was deep in numbers when he heard a chime. Instead of the doorbell he'd expected, it came from his phone.

"Hey, Mom," he answered, glancing at the wall clock. "You're supposed to be here in five minutes. Is everything all right?"

"Everything is fine, mijo, but something's come up and I won't be able to join you today."

Alex shifted forward and settled his laptop on the coffee table.

"What? Why?"

Eddie perked up at his tone, and Alex smiled at his nephew to reassure him nothing was wrong.

His mother issued a little cough, and an idea began to form.

"Oh, it seems I got the date wrong and I already made plans to have lunch with the girls. Normally, I'd skip and come with you and the kids, but we have the library fundraiser coming up and I'd really hate to leave them high and dry. Especially since I'm the most organized one and Lord knows how they'd manage without me."

Alex rolled his eyes up to the ceiling and pressed his lips together in a line.

"Mom. If you're the most organized one, how did you get the dates mixed up in your calendar? I've seen the thing. It's color coded and emails you reminders. And they pop up on your phone!"

Rosa Trevino sighed, then released a giggle. "Well, I'm getting older you know, Alex, and I can't be expected to get everything right all the time, can I? Even I make mistakes."

He closed his laptop and stood to pace the room. "Except you don't."

When she didn't respond, he added, "I know what this is, Mom. But you know Gina and I have been spending plenty of time together without your *intervention*, so there's no need for you to skip out on plans to push us together or something equally ridiculous."

When she spoke again, her tone was serious. "If what you're suggesting were true, *hypothetically*, then yes, you'd be right. I have seen you spending lots of time together, and I couldn't be happier about it." She paused.

"So what's the problem then?"

"Well, it's not just you any longer, darling. You've got Eddie and Carmen to think about."

His heart sank. How had she called out exactly the thing that had been bothering him the past week, when he hadn't been able to see it himself?

"I know that, and I'd never do anything to hurt those kids. I'm being careful."

Was he, though?

"I know you are, son. And I know Gina will be wonderful with them, but she needs to spend more time around them so she can get to know them better and see if she wants to—"

"Please don't say it, Mom. We're just getting to know each other again. I'm not ready to think about that, and she's not either."

His mom was silent for several seconds, which gave him a chance to digest the words he'd said aloud. No, he wouldn't force Gina into loving his kids, into loving him, into becoming a family. But he desperately wished for her to want those things, and he didn't know how long he could stand not knowing whether or not she ever would.

"I won't say that." She pulled in a breath. "I will say this, though—she's worth the trouble, Alex. And I can't speak for her, but I think she's ready for something real. But she hasn't had a lot to rely on in this life, and she might not know how to accept the idea of building a future with you, even if she wants to."

He closed his eyes and then opened them, watching as Carmen joined Eddie on the big recliner, tucking her small form into his side. Eddie squirmed and then relented, putting an arm around her.

Those kids were precious; they were his world now.

What he wanted mattered, but not as much as what they *needed*. Dependability. A stable home. People they could count on.

Which hadn't really been in Gina's wheelhouse up to now.

"Thanks, Mom. I know. I have a lot to think about."

"Sure. That's what I'm here for. But, Alex?"

"Yeah?"

"Think with your heart too, not just your brain."

"I will," he said.

But after hanging up, he wasn't sure it was true. He'd done plenty of thinking with his heart in the past, and things hadn't turned out too well.

This time he'd have to be sure before giving it away again.

The weather was on its best behavior that morning, showing off its finest gentle breeze, foreshadowing a sunny but pleasant day ahead as Gina took her time strolling toward the ranch house.

Her heart was bubbly and light, filled with champagne fizz as she pictured the hours ahead. She'd been nervous when Alex first suggested the day trip, thinking it would just be the four of them. The idea of going out in Peach Leaf like that, like a family unit, gave her pause. She enjoyed Carmen and Eddie—they were sweet kids and she'd been getting more and more comfortable every time she'd seen them since she and Alex had started... whatever it was they were doing. But she wasn't ready for anyone—especially not the kids—to get the impression she was a permanent part of their family. Not yet. She needed time to get used to the idea herself before others started drawing conclusions.

So when Alex had said Rosa was coming to help look after the kids, and they were meeting up with Van and her family, Gina had been flooded with relief.

When she got to the house, she opened the door and called out a greeting, just as she had in the old days. It felt good to just walk in as though she belonged there. So good she wondered whether it might be true, that she *did* belong.

She and Alex had been spending a lot of time together, and yes it was incredible. All the things she'd loved about him when they were young remained in place, but other things had changed for the better. Where their intimacy had been urgent and ravenous in those first years together, now it was attentive, giving, unrushed, yet the passion remained.

But she knew they were both avoiding a discussion about how to move forward from here. When they were together, unspoken questions hovered in the quiet aftermath. And she still wasn't sure how she felt about entering into something permanent. Alex, Carmen, and Eddie came as a package. Was she ready to accept a role as the kids' mom?

She knew things were different this time. If she stepped into a real relationship with Alex, she couldn't walk away again without causing harm, this time to two wonderful kids who'd already been through enough.

But even if she wanted to, *could* she walk away? Or was she already in too deep, regardless of her lingering uncertainties?

"Hey, Gina," Alex greeted as she walked into the living room.

Eddie and Carmen were nestled together in the recliner, Eddie looking slightly annoyed with the bundle at his side, and Alex was hunched over a laptop that he closed and set down when he saw her.

When their eyes met, his lips broke into a know-ing grin that brought back images from two nights ago. Bare flesh, rumpled sheets, kisses so fiery she felt warmth rise up the back of her neck until she had to look away.

"You look amazing," he said.

She scoffed. "Jeez, Alex. I'm wearing old shorts and a T-shirt, and my hair is a mess as usual…"

"Nevertheless," he said, rising. He closed the space between them and wrapped her in his arms, where her head fit just under his chin. She breathed in lemony soap, coffee and cinnamon. Alex. Her Alex.

Soft giggles erupted from the recliner.

Alex pulled back and turned toward the kids in mock surprise. "What's so funny?" he asked.

"Nothing!" Carmen said, laughing harder.

"Oh yeah?" he called out, winking at Gina be-fore letting her go.

He took big, slow steps toward the kids, arms outstretched in an imitation of a giant.

Carmen's laughter exploded into squeals with each step Alex took toward them, while Eddie tried to maintain his cool factor and failed, even-tually giving over to his own adorable chuckles.

Gina watched in awe. Alex had always liked kids, had always been confident he wanted to be a father. Unlike her, he'd never struggled with the idea, but that made sense because he came from a family where kids were treasured and treated like a gift, rather than a burden. Gina wondered if she would be less afraid of motherhood if she'd grown up in such an environment, or if it was normal for women to worry about having children. And her own struggle seemed particularly challenging because she wasn't exactly choosing between a career or children, which seemed to be the only acceptable debate if one were to trust the media and the comments even strangers felt were their right to make. To her dismay, some people seemed to think it was okay to ask any woman over thirty or so why she didn't have kids, as if it were an obligation rather than a choice. Gina had never heard anyone ask a man the same.

Besides, she didn't even *have* a career to consider at the moment. She just flat out wasn't sure what she wanted. And she'd never thought to ask any of her friends because, whether they did or didn't become mothers, they all seemed to just *know* which path was right for them.

Gina envied that kind of certainty.

"Help, Miss Gina!" Carmen cried out through fits of laughter. "Save us from the tickle monster!"

And then there was Carmen, she thought, who

didn't care whether Gina wanted to be a mom or not. She just wanted someone to pay attention to her, to see her.

Eddie squirmed away from the pile and rolled his eyes at Gina, even as he bit his bottom lip to stifle more giggles.

As Gina pushed aside her worries and raised her arms, taking her own giant monster stance to join in the fun, the only thought she had was that in moments like these, the choice was easy.

If only it were always that simple.

Chapter Eleven

"What do you mean she's not coming?" Gina asked after the laughter had cooled and Alex rousted the kids to get their shoes on so they could leave for the wildflower center.

He turned to her with a sheepish expression. "All she'd say was that she mixed up the dates in her calendar. Apparently she double-booked our day out with a library fundraiser planning lunch."

Gina had a feeling there was more to the story, but Alex just shrugged and proceeded to grab water bottles and snacks, which he tucked into a backpack.

"A mix-up, huh?" she asked. "How is that even

possible? Your mom's calendar is more reliable than the rotation of the Earth."

Alex cringed. "I know. Tell me about it." He slung the backpack over one shoulder and raised his arms innocently. "But that's what she told me."

"Do you think someone's playing matchmaker?" she asked.

"What's a matchmaker?" Carmen asked, skipping into the kitchen.

"Uh, it's a…" Alex's eyes darted to Gina.

"It's a person who introduces people to each other and tries to get them to be friends."

Carmen bit her lip and tilted her head to the side, sending one of her pigtails tumbling over her little shoulder. "Miss Gina and me are friends now. Did we have a matchmaker?"

"I guess you did, in a way," Alex answered, holding Gina's gaze.

Carmen raced over and wrapped her arms around Gina's legs, squeezing. "I'm glad," she said, closing her eyes as she tucked her head into Gina's side.

Reaching down, she ran a hand over the little girl's hair. Sweet moments like this one had the power to soften her resolve, but they weren't enough to push her in one direction or the other regarding parenthood. Carmen was affectionate by nature and shared it freely with others, but she was only six years old. Gina knew from her college student teaching practicum that as kids grew, the questions became harder and the answers less readily accepted.

How could she respond to tough queries about things like climate change and child hunger and poverty when she didn't have those answers herself? The world seemed so unjust at times, and she knew that Carmen and Eddie would someday want to know why. If she chose to stay, to partner with Alex to raise them—a thought she was surprised to even find herself considering—how would she know what to say about the truly hard stuff when they asked?

She and Sophie had grown up wondering some of those very same things, and even in adulthood, Gina hadn't been able to find satisfactory answers.

But for now... "I'm glad too," she said to the little one hugging her.

Alex was watching them with an unreadable expression, and Gina wondered if he had some of the same thoughts she did. After all, these kids had come to him unexpectedly. She wondered whether he would want more children in the future or if he felt like his family was already complete.

"Okay, little monsters, let's get going," he finally said, herding them out to the truck.

When Eddie and Carmen were settled in the back seat, he turned to Gina.

"Are you okay with this? They can be a handful, and if you're not comfortable coming along, no hard feelings."

As much as they both probably wanted to believe that, it couldn't possibly be true and she knew it.

Buckling her seat belt to avoid eye contact, she took her time responding as he started the truck and checked the mirrors. "Yeah, I think so," she said, pulling in a breath. "Things with us have been good—"

"They've been amazing," he interjected, reaching over to take her hand, which had begun to tremble.

Unable to look at him, she stared down into her lap. "They have been. I can't argue with that."

He squeezed her hand, and she forced herself to meet his eyes, afraid that doing so might make the emotion welling up in her chest far more difficult to shield from him.

"And I do want to spend more time with you, Alex—" she glanced toward the back seat "—and them. I'm just... I'm worried I'm not going to be very good at it."

"Well, there is one trick," he said, his brows knit in exaggerated seriousness.

"What's that?" she asked, playing along.

"Just be you. I promise if you give it a chance, you're going to be okay."

Placing a hand on the steering wheel, he turned

a key in the ignition with the other and the truck rumbled to life.

"I know it'll work on them," he added with a wink, "because it's definitely working on me."

When they got to the Peach Leaf Wildflower Center, Van and Darian were hanging out near the entrance with their kiddos, six-year-old Tanya and ten-year-old Caleb. The second Alex released her from her seat belt, Carmen burst into a jog to get to Tanya while Eddie and Caleb waved shy hellos and started what sounded to Gina like a very mature conversation about an upcoming project at school.

"They're peas in a pod, aren't they?" Van asked, giving Gina a friendly wave. Lovely spiral curls surrounded her face, held loosely back by a floral-patterned scarf that picked up the blue of her T-shirt. She wore the same kind smile that had made Gina feel so welcome in her shop.

"Ten going on forty," Alex added. "Before you know it, we'll be consulting them about 401(k)s."

"You joke," Darian said, "but Caleb's already started asking me if he can sit in when I file this year's taxes."

Van rolled her eyes, and her husband tossed her an adoring smile. "Oh, he has not. Don't pay this guy a lick of attention."

"How's it been going otherwise, guys?" Alex

reached out to Darian for a handshake before folding Van into a friendly half hug.

"It's been good," Darian said. "Can't complain." He tucked his hands into the pockets of his jeans and looked at his wife with warm brown eyes. "And Van here just got featured in a Houston magazine about the best craft stores in the state, not that she's told anyone in town."

She gave her husband a mock glare, but even a fool could see that she was delighted by his praise.

Gina felt a pang of envy. She couldn't begrudge these good people their obvious love and happiness, but she wished for a moment that she could have the same. Alex glanced her way and their eyes met briefly. Did he feel that way too?

"It's just a little local magazine," Van said, brushing off the attention with a wave of a hand. "I doubt anyone will even read the piece."

"Right," Darian said, deadpan. "A little local magazine from a major city with a hefty, loyal readership. Is that why the phone's been ringing off the hook and your emails have tripled in the past week?" He pointed a thumb at her. "This one," he said, shaking his head. "Modest to a fault."

"Now you sound like my mother," Van said, poking him with her elbow.

"Who is a lovely woman, by the way," Darian added, making the others laugh.

"So where's Rosa?" Van asked, glancing around

the group and over toward Alex's truck. "I thought she was joining us today?"

"Oh, uh, she couldn't make it," Alex said, absently scratching the back of his head. He glanced briefly at Gina as if to say, *not this again.*

She stifled a chuckle. This was only one of a handful of downsides of small-town life. But then again, Gina thought as she watched Alex laughing with his friends, was that such a bad thing? Could she do this? Let people into her life on a permanent basis? What was there to be afraid of now? Her school-era bullies were grown and had serious problems of their own. Her sister had built a life in Peach Leaf and wanted Gina to put down roots so that they could be closer and make up for lost time. And then there was Alex...

She didn't regret the adventurous path she'd taken, but since being home and experiencing true companionship again, she had to admit that the nomadic life had become a little lonely. So if she hadn't found happiness there, and she couldn't find it here, then bigger questions remained: What was she running from? And, more importantly, what did she really want out of this one life?

Van noticed the exchange between Alex and Gina, but said only, "Well, give Miss Rosa my love, and tell her we missed her."

Alex nodded, appearing grateful that Van hadn't pressed the issue.

"Well, let's get to it!" Darian said, clapping his hands together eagerly. "I can't wait to take this year's bluebonnet pictures."

"Dad!" Caleb groaned. "Why do we have to do those every year? They're exactly the same every time and they're sooo lame."

"Because it's a Texas tradition!" Darian protested to a chorus of groaning from the kids.

Eddie issued a little chuckle. "My mom used to make us do them, too," he said, looking down at his sneakers. "I kinda missed it last year. Even though I guess it *is* pretty lame."

Alex caught Gina's eye and then spoke to Eddie. "How about we continue the tradition this year, bud?"

The little boy looked up with a crooked grin. "Really?"

"Of course," Alex said, wrapping a hand over Eddie's shoulder. "I think your mom would like that."

"Okay," Eddie said, then paused and gave a slight frown. "But what if we do it different this time?"

"What did you have in mind?" Van asked. "Despite the kids' protests, Darian's an excellent photographer," she said to Gina, taking her husband's hand.

Eddie cocked his head to the side. "Well, I really

like *gaillardia pulchella* better than plain old blue-bonnets. Can we take pictures with those instead?"

Van and Darian traded warm smiles. "Of course, Ed," Darian said. "Quick question, though…what the heck is *gaillardia pulchella*?"

Everyone laughed and Eddie smiled broadly, happy to share his knowledge with the group. "It's a Firewheel flower," he said. "Duh."

"Duh!" Carmen repeated, earning yet another eye roll from her very patient brother.

"Oh, I love those!" Gina said. "They're so beau-tiful."

Eddie's cheeks glowed at her praise for his fa-vorite flower, and the two shared a grin.

"Let's grab tickets then," Van suggested. "Be-fore it gets too crowded." After delegating the job to Alex and her husband, she joined Gina to wait for the guys.

"So," she said, amusement glinting in her hazel eyes, "I haven't seen my best bud in a while, and he owes me a mystery novel exchange. Any idea what might be keeping him? I suppose it *could* be a coincidence that he turned scarce right about the time you got to town, but I have my doubts."

Cursing her pale skin as the telltale heat of a blush crept up her neck, Gina looked away. But it was too late. A smile had already spread across her lips and Van hadn't missed it, which didn't surprise her because Van seemed like a woman who didn't miss much of anything.

"I see," Van said, expertly herding the kids toward a nearby picnic table. She patted the empty space on the bench seat next to her, and Gina obliged. "I would make a fuss about it, except—" she tossed a glance over to where Alex and Darian stood near the middle of a growing ticket line, chatting animatedly "—I've never seen him so happy."

"It's… I don't think that has anything to do with me," Gina protested lamely.

Without saying a word, Van raised a single eyebrow. "You think I don't know my own friend well enough to see when something's changed, and figure out what caused it?"

Gina was smart enough to know when she'd been bested. "All right, I get where you're coming from, and at this point you know him better than I do, but it's not…what we're doing is nothing serious."

"Have you told him that?" Van asked. "And for the record, I doubt I know him better than you do. From what I've heard, which is a lot, the two of you had something pretty special. Once in a lifetime, even. I get the impression no one could ever know him the way you do, time apart notwithstanding."

Her tone was firm but nonjudgmental. She was looking out for her close friend, just as Gina would have done for her sister, and Gina couldn't take offense at that loving protectiveness.

"Not in so many words," she said, feeling a little bit ashamed, for which she could only blame herself.

"Well, I'm not going to tell you what to do," Van said, "but I'm duty bound by the best friend code to say this—I'd hate to see him get his heart broken."

Again.

The word sat painfully in the air between them, though Alex's friend had been kind enough not to say it aloud.

Knowing that her features were the sort that gave everything away whether she wanted them to or not, Gina decided to just go for honesty. "I don't want to hurt anyone," she said. "This was unexpected for us both, and we haven't really discussed it beyond acknowledging that we'll have to address the future at some point."

Van nodded. "I get that." She lowered her voice to a whisper, so the kids wouldn't hear. "Figuring things out would be easier if others weren't in the picture, too, huh?"

"It would," Gina said, appreciating Van's candor. "What happened to his family has definitely complicated things, but there's no use in dwelling on that. Alex has always done the right thing by his kin, so I wouldn't expect anything else from him."

"Always," Van agreed. "Even to his own detriment."

Gina's ears perked up. "What do you mean?"

Van cut her a look of disbelief. "You don't need me to tell you how hard it was for him after you left. He made the choice he thought was best at the time, but it wasn't without cost. I can't speak for him, of course, but I get the sense that if he opened up about it, he would probably tell you that he's still not sure whether choosing to stay here was worth losing you."

"Actually," Gina said, her voice shaky, "I think I did need to hear that."

While thankful, she couldn't help but wish the words had come from Alex himself.

"Well, if it helps… I wasn't around when it happened, obviously, but from what everyone says, he was gutted by your loss. And when I met him, you were one of the subjects he talked about the most."

"I'm sorry," Gina said with humor. "Listening to him go on about me must have been a pain. I'm surprised you wanted to hang around him after that."

Van tossed her head back and laughed, sending her light brown curls swaying.

Her physical features seemed to match the woman within, Gina thought. Sunshine and warmth and delight. They were lovely traits, and Gina could imagine that most people who met Van would want to be friends with her.

"Well, we also talked about books a lot, to be fair," Van said. "But yeah, I could tell he still had feelings for you, and I don't believe they've faded."

"Alex could have done a hell of a lot worse in the friendship department," Gina said. "I'm glad he's had you looking out for him these past several years."

"Well, he's pretty special," she said, regarding Gina. "But then, you already know that."

With a solemn smile of agreement as the conversation dwindled, Gina admired her surroundings.

The sun, hidden behind a veil of morning clouds, gave off warmth without being overwhelming. Hummingbirds with their tiny, fairylike wings and butterflies in every color of the rainbow flitted back and forth between flower beds and miniature potted gardens, eager to taste a little of everything. She imagined it was a veritable feast for all manner of creatures, between the decorative plants at the center's entryway to the treasures that no doubt lined the walking trails they would soon set out on. It promised to be a beautiful day, with Alex and the kids by her side.

So why couldn't she relax and enjoy it? What was it about sweet days like the one ahead, full of so many of the fine, simple things life had to offer, that made her feel so anxious?

Sophie had asked the same thing a few nights ago, when Gina invited her over for dinner, fresh from helping Alex with after school pickup and snacks.

"I can see you're having a great time with him," her sister had commented. "Why can't you just let go of the past and let yourself be happy in the present?"

Why indeed?

Something Rosa had said resonated again in the back of her mind. Maybe the older woman had been right. Maybe her parents' inadequacies weren't her fault, and their inability to love her properly wasn't a reflection of her worth. Maybe she did deserve to be loved—fully, unconditionally, permanently—by someone else.

By Alex?

Did she still love him?

But even as she asked herself the silent question, she knew the answer. There was no *still*, because she'd never stopped. This time her affection for him hadn't shown up in fireworks or big revelations. It had simply reignited from an ember, glowing softly but persistently all the while, waiting to be rekindled as she'd sought answers beyond her humble beginnings.

"Here they are," Van called out as Darian and

Alex came toward them bearing the goods. "All set?"

"Yep," Alex said, handing Van and Gina little neon strips of plastic with adhesive ends. "We've just got to get wristbands on these knuckleheads and we're good to go."

"Easier said than done," Van answered with a wink before gathering up the kids, all four of whom wriggled with pent-up energy.

"I want Miss Gina to put mine on!" Carmen shouted.

Warmth rippled through her as Carmen held out her tiny arm and Gina circled it with the band. She closed the plastic snaps, and the little darling gave her a quick hug before skipping back to join Tanya and their brothers.

Despite her misgivings about children, it was undeniably nice to be liked by them, Carmen and Eddie in particular. To have garnered the kids' approval, for them to care about spending time with her when their world was full of shiny diversions, gave her more satisfaction than she would have guessed.

"Feeling pretty smug, are you?" Alex asked, sparking a different sort of heat inside her, his breath near enough to tickle her ear. "You know they ask every night you're not already there if you can come for dinner. Pretty soon, they'll be bored with me and you'll be the main attraction."

He nudged her shoulder with his own. "Not that I can blame them. You are pretty distracting."

"Hush," she scolded, equal parts anxious and pleased that he wasn't ashamed to show her affection among his friends.

"As if Van and Darian don't already know," he said. "They're my best buds. They know when I'm fond of something."

She looked up and he captured her full attention.

"Or someone."

"Are you?" she asked, lifting her chin. "Fond of me?

"More than I can say."

He reached out and wrapped his fingers gently around her wrist, sending the barest hint of arousal down her spine.

"Could you try?" she asked, startled by the immediacy of her flirty response. Where had that come from?

He leaned in so close that she could see the gilded flecks in his dark brown eyes and feel the warmth radiating from his sun-kissed skin. "I think that would be ill-advised, given present company," he said, his voice low and rich, suggestive of things not fit for a public space. "But the next time I have you to myself," he whispered, "I plan to show you."

With that, he raised her wrist, planted a kiss at

the spot where her pulse beat against her skin, then wrapped the neon band around it and fastened it.

He gave her an incredible smile and stepped back toward the group, leaving her flushed, breathless and wondering how she would manage to hide the feelings he'd shaken up. Deliberately.

The scoundrel.

"And what's this one?" Gina asked his nephew, pointing to a bloom with hot pink petals drooping downward around a bright golden center.

"That's *echinacea purpurea*," Eddie answered with an expert's confidence.

"And for those in the back?" Alex asked, earning a grin from Gina.

Eddie blinked at him in confusion and Alex chuckled, then asked, "What's the name for those of us who aren't so great at botany?"

"Oh, yes. It's a purple cornflower," Eddie clarified.

"You said echinacea. Would that be the same as the kind that's supposed to be good for a cold?" Gina asked.

"That's the one," Eddie said. "Good job, Miss Gina."

Alex glanced over just in time to watch her absorb the compliment. Her eyes glittered with a hint of moisture, and her lips pressed together as she tried to curtail obvious emotion.

"Well, I have a good teacher," she said.

It made his heart swell to see two people he adored interacting this way. An introvert, Eddie had never been particularly outgoing, a fact that his family accepted without trying to pressure or change him. Alex made sure that the kiddo saw his few but close friends as often as possible, so that Eddie didn't get lonely or miss out on important social interaction, but he didn't often seek out new connections. That's why it was so cool to see his growing bond with Gina. It seemed effortless and natural for them both.

And it gave Alex hope.

Gina had always been so beloved by his family, and that seemed to extend to his late brother's and sister-in-law's children as well.

His children, Alex reminded himself. They were his now, a fact that he warmed to more and more each day, helped along by the idea that a little family was forming around them.

But did she feel the same way? He wanted to ask her, but couldn't seem to find the words.

Eddie reached up and took Alex's hand, pulling him from his thoughts. Then his nephew took Gina's hand in the other, one on each side.

Gina's eyes glittered, and she turned to swipe at her face with her free hand.

"Are you okay?" Carmen asked. She'd been skipping in a circle around them, singing to herself as they wandered along the nature trail, but now her senses honed in on Gina's poorly hidden tears.

"Oh, I'm fine," Gina said, smiling broadly. "Just very, very happy."

"I'm happy too!" Carmen squealed before hopping off toward the Greens, who were just up ahead on the path.

"So am I," Eddie said, his tone matter-of-fact. "I guess that makes three of us."

Alex caught Gina's light brown eyes over the top of Eddie's head. "Four," Alex amended. "Make that four of us."

The group walked the trails in no hurry at all, admiring the different, beautifully curated gardens. There was a wetland pond area featuring aquatic plants that grew only in water or water-soaked earth. Tanya and Caleb even spotted a couple of toads, and a harmless ribbon snake nearly sent Carmen into a frenzy before Van calmed her down by explaining that this specific type of snake was nonpoisonous.

Alex's favorite was a meadow area saturated with wildflowers and native trees like the ones his parents had nurtured and allowed to flourish on the ranch. Blues, yellows, oranges and reds dotted the grassland, and Alex was certain that he'd never seen a more beautiful sight than that of Gina standing in the middle, eyes closed as she spun in a circle, golden curls swirling around her face. She seemed wholly unconcerned whether anyone was watching or not.

But watch he did, heart twisting with adoration and something else he tried to ignore…a sense of foreboding. For a few hours that day, Alex had everything in the world he'd ever wished for. His niece and nephew, his best friends and the woman he'd loved since the first time he'd spoken to her. It was incredible and perfect and yet so fragile.

She had no idea how much power she held, how easily she could take this away from him if she chose to leave again.

But he knew better now. He knew what it was to lose her and this time, if she wanted to go, he would ask her to stay. No, he'd do better than that…

This time, he would fight for her.

Chapter Twelve

"All right, who's hungry?" came Van's voice over the din of tired kids and worn-out adults, all getting a little grumpy as their stomachs grumbled and the day grew hotter, the sun rising high and escaping the earlier cloud cover.

"I'm famished," answered Darian, placing a hand over his dad-bod tummy.

"I could eat," said Eddie.

"Me too!" said Carmen, Tanya and Caleb all at once.

"Okay, then," Alex said, making his way toward Gina. "Have you been to the café here?"

She shook her head. "No, I haven't. Soph says it's great."

"She's right. They've got something for every-one. There's a vegan menu and gluten free options, and— What?" he asked, searching her eyes for the reason behind her wry smile.

"Nothing. Just impressed by my soft-hearted cowboy who cares about food choices for vegans and those with food sensitivities."

Heart pounding, he'd missed most of what she'd said, hung up on one word.

"Did you say *my* cowboy?"

A hand flew to her lips, and she covered them as if to prevent anything else from escaping.

"I suppose I did," she said.

He reached forward to tuck a wayward curl be-hind her ear, letting his fingers brush the soft skin at her temple.

"Is that okay?" she asked.

"It's more than okay. It's—"

"Gina? Alex?"

She turned, leaving his hand hovering in midair.

"What are you guys doing here?" Sophie asked, her cheeks pink.

Whether it was from the now-blazing sun or the fact that Jesse was standing next to her, holding her hand, Alex couldn't be sure.

He watched as Gina's eyes fell to Sophie's and his cousin's hands, then met her sister's. Sophie and Jesse pulled apart as if an electric shock had separated them, but Alex knew instantly another kind of spark had gone off between them.

"Just enjoying a day out," Alex said, breaking the tension. "It was gorgeous until about an hour ago." He turned to his uncharacteristically speechless cousin. "Hey, Jess, how's it going?"

"It's, uh, good." Jesse swallowed, tucking his hands into the pockets of his shorts. "Great, actually."

It was kind of funny to watch. It wasn't easy to fluster laid-back, carefree Jesse, but this was sure doing it.

He glanced at Gina, and they both broke out in grins.

"You guys want to join us for lunch?" he asked, arm out to include Van, Darian and the kids, who were waiting a few yards ahead.

Sophie's eyes were on her shoes but Gina's lips had spread into a wide grin, and Alex could see that she was happy for her sister.

"Sure, why not?" she said, barely above a whisper.

She looked at Jesse, and Alex wondered how he'd missed it before. The two were enamored with each other; it was right there in front of him. Gina had mentioned something about the two of them the other day when they'd gotten together for margaritas, but Alex had been so focused on the idea of her moving into the cabin that he hadn't paid much attention. As he sifted back through the last few months, it all started to make sense, and he couldn't wait to be alone with Gina and pick over this fascinating development.

"What's the holdup over here?" Darian asked, coming over to see what was keeping them. "Oh, hey, Jesse, Sophie," he greeted nonchalantly, not noticing or caring that they were obviously together.

Alex chuckled, admiring how easygoing his friend always seemed to be.

"Nothing," Gina said. "Let's get some food."

Sophie and Jesse exchanged a sheepish glance and came together again, shoulder to shoulder, clearly a little relieved that they didn't have to hide their obvious affection. Alex suspected Sophie had been a little surprised to find she had real feelings for his cousin, who could be a bit of a rogue. And, most likely, Jesse just didn't know what to do with himself in a real relationship, having spent most of his adult life playing the field with little regard for serious commitment.

Maybe they had all finally grown up, he thought,

pleased with the idea. And, maybe, now they could all move forward, better than before.

Half an hour later, their expanded party was seated at an outdoor table on the covered patio of the wildflower center's café. Fans buzzed overhead, making the heat more bearable. There had been a debate over whether or not to eat indoors where it was much cooler, but Alex and Van had agreed that doing so would be unkind to other diners, what with four hangry kids and Darian and Jesse, who were both chatterboxes and could get loud when talking about their favorite Austin soccer team.

Fortified with icy glasses of sweet tea and a basket of garlic kettle chips making its way around the table, the group waited—some patiently, others, notably Carmen and Tanya, not so much— for lunch to arrive. Alex and Gina had ordered a turkey sandwich with Havarti, arugula and a tart and sweet fig spread to share, while Van enjoyed a banh mi and Darian a veggie sandwich with aioli spread. Tanya, Carmen and Caleb each had grilled cheese on whole wheat and Eddie chose a Greek salad paired with pita and hummus.

"So, how long have you two been seeing each

other?" Van asked, glancing between Jesse and Sophie.

The two shared a look and blushed immediately.

"Uh, a couple of months, I guess." Sophie said quietly.

"Two months and eleven days," Jesse announced with a wide, shining grin.

Obviously delighted at this attention to detail and what it signified, Sophie surprised them all by leaning over to kiss Jesse's cheek. And the way he looked at Gina's sister in return could only be described as love.

It was, Alex noted with a flutter in his chest, exactly the way he looked at Gina these days.

"Well, there must be something in the water," Van said, tossing him a look.

"I had no idea!" Darian said, making everyone laugh as Van gave her husband a soft, loving shoulder punch.

"It's okay, sweetheart," she said. "You've got me."

"Best thing that ever happened to me," Darian agreed.

They ate the rest of the food with verve, putting a temporary halt to the chatter. Then they hung around for another half hour, catching up, before leaving the café.

Rather than being sleepy and weighed down by carbs, the kids wanted to check out the play area, so they agreed to do that before heading home. On the way back to the cars, Eddie said, "Hey! We forgot to take pictures."

"You're right, bud," Alex said, turning to Darian. "Still up for it?"

"Of course," Darian said amiably. "I've got my camera right here." He patted his back pocket. "Van got me a new phone, and the camera's just as good as my mirrorless."

"Great," Alex said. "Let's do it."

They retraced their steps back to the meadow Alex had admired earlier and decided on a few shots they wanted to get. First, one with all four kids, then one with each family's pair, then Darian showed Alex what settings to use and how to frame them so that he could capture Darian and Van.

Just as Alex thought they were finished and ready to head out, Van grabbed his elbow. "Not so fast," she said.

"Huh?"

She nodded at Gina, who stood to the side, avoiding the fray. "I want one of the two of you."

"That's okay," Gina said. "I'm sure y'all are tired and ready to get the kids home."

"Nonsense," Van argued, giving Alex a little shove. "Go and stand over there, you two."

He tossed Gina a look of apology and mouthed *sorry.* She attempted a grin, but it came out looking like nausea instead. Taking her hand, he led her to the middle of the field where she'd stood earlier. She was even more beautiful up close, the sun glinting off her curls, eyes almond-colored in the bright light, lips and cheeks rosy from a day of sun. Before they'd even turned, Alex heard the phone click, then he completely blocked out the sound as he stared into Gina's lovely face.

The sun bore down on the back of his neck, but the heat coming from light-years away wasn't nearly as warm as the heat welling up inside him.

She was everything he remembered, but so much more, and suddenly he ached to tell her.

"Gina, I think I—"

"Shh," she said. "Don't say anything."

And with that, she reached up with both hands, cupping his face as she stood on tiptoes to bring her lips against his.

"Now that's more like it!" Van shouted, as Darian, Jesse, Sophie and the kids began to clap and holler with glee.

Gina began to giggle, breaking the kiss, and Alex folded her into his arms, giving the audience a wave, which just made them more jubilant and therefore louder.

"You gave me a second chance after all," he said, referring to their botched first attempt only a week before.

So little time had passed, but it felt like he'd had her back for longer. Yet, even if she stayed for a lifetime, it could never be enough. He wanted her there, by his side, beyond forever.

"I did," she said, eyes glistening. "Will you do the same for me?" Her meaning went well beyond the kiss.

"I will," he said. "I'm not giving up this time."

And with that he bent to kiss her again, which he planned to do as often as possible, as long as she'd let him.

"I had the best day ever," Carmen said as Gina lifted her from the back seat of Alex's truck.

The little girl's tawny skin was warm and flushed in spite of the sunblock Alex had slathered on and the sweet little pink baseball cap he'd made her wear, to much protest. Gina was certain the kids would be tired after the long day, and sure enough they'd both napped on the way back to the ranch.

"It was pretty awesome, wasn't it," Gina agreed,

taking Carmen's outstretched hand to lead her inside the house while Alex grabbed his backpack, trailing Eddie up to the porch.

She tossed Alex a glance over her shoulder and returned his smile, remembering the feel of his lips on hers in the middle of that beautiful meadow. It had been like a dream, one she'd never wanted to wake up from, and for several incredible moments it had indeed seemed possible for it to go on forever.

But the day was coming to a close, and they were back to real life. And, despite their chemistry, those delicious kisses, and a week of intimacy that had awakened her body to pleasure she hadn't known before, she and Alex still hadn't addressed the future.

Using the small workspace Jesse had built for her in the cabin, she'd been plenty busy when she hadn't been spending time with Alex. Upholstery orders had trickled into her email, first at a slow pace, then increasing as, she supposed, word-of-mouth spread around town. If she allowed herself to hope, she could admit that her business was growing, and if it kept up the steady pace, she could see herself making a living in the near future. Doing what she loved. Thanks to her own elbow grease, and to Alex and his kindhearted mom, who were doing as they always had—treating her like family.

How could she ever show her gratitude?

Maybe by sticking around, a small voice whispered inside her.

That little voice wasn't wrong, and her heart leaped at the idea, which came as a surprise. It would mean putting down roots, building her client list, making a home out of her beloved little cabin. It could also mean committing to a relationship with Alex, and to Carmen and Eddie.

Her heart lifted. *I want that*, she thought. *I really do*.

She wasn't ready for the kids to think of calling her *mom* or anything, not just yet. But she did feel ready to tell Alex how she felt. And she hoped he felt the same, but she was prepared to hear and accept his wishes too. Having grown closer to him and the kids, she knew they could build a life together, and she was ready to find out what that might look like for all of them.

"After bath time, can I spend the night at Miss Gina's cabin?" Carmen asked, twirling a lock of thick brown hair around her finger.

Gina paused and turned to Alex. She nodded, giving him the space to answer. He raised an eyebrow.

"I don't see why not," he said tentatively. "If it's okay with her."

Letting out a slow breath, she responded. "Sounds like fun."

"Yay!" Carmen shouted, her little hands moving as she bounced up and down.

"I'd like to come too," Eddie said, reaching the door. Alex opened it, ushering them inside.

"Well," Alex said, catching Gina's eye, "why don't we all spend the night? If that's okay."

She bit her bottom lip, fully aware what this meant. If the kids stayed over and Alex did too, it would affix something permanent in their world. Something they couldn't go back on. It would mean that serious discussion about the future would have to happen as soon as possible. Being responsible for the kids came first for Alex and, increasingly, for her, so they would need to be clear and open with each other about expectations from now on.

Was she ready?

"Yes," she said, feeling even surer as she spoke the word aloud. "It's okay."

Her heart lightened as Alex smiled, and she began to plan. They could have milk and some of the chocolate chip cookies Rosa had brought over the previous afternoon. Then they could snuggle up on the couch and watch a movie of the kids' choosing. Gina would set up there for the night, and the kids and Alex could take the bed. It would be fun.

The four of them went inside and she helped where she felt comfortable, brushing Carmen's hair and getting her little pink suitcase packed with pajamas. Alex and Eddie packed a bag together, and, after a light dinner since everyone agreed they were still full from lunch, they got back into the truck and headed for Gina's cabin.

The sun had begun its descent by the time they reached her door, and soft, golden light bathed her still-empty flower beds, which looked inviting now, rather than daunting.

"You can tell me if you've had a change of heart," Alex reassured as they got out of the truck. "I know it's a lot, and I don't want to pressure you."

"No, it's really okay," she said. "More than okay. I'm excited to have you guys spend the night, and for whatever comes after that." She willed him to understand what she meant, and it seemed he did, as he came around to her side of the truck and pressed a kiss onto her cheek.

Later that night, after the movie, Alex and Carmen were snoozing. Gina thought Eddie might be as well because his breathing was even, but he was on the other side of the couch so she couldn't quite see to be sure. Deciding she needed a little fuel before rousing the three of them, she went to the kitchen and made a cup of tea. When she returned to sit in the recliner, Eddie raised up on his elbow and gave her a grin.

She patted the space next to her on the large seat and he ambled over, tucking his form against her.

That was one of the things she hadn't been aware of, just how comforting little warm bodies were, how nice it felt to hold a small hand or to be hugged by them. So nice, she wasn't sure she could ever give it up.

"What did you think of the wildflower center?" she asked.

Eddie squinted his eyes and bit his lip in thought. "I liked it," he said after a few seconds. "It was a little bit too hot, and my grilled cheese sandwich wasn't as good as the ones my dad used to make, but it was nice to see Caleb and all the plants."

Her heart did a little dance, and she resisted the urge to reach out and hug him, knowing Eddie liked his space. The young man was so present in the world, so careful in his actions and his speech. He would grow up to be a fine person, and if he ever chose to be, he would make a wonderful partner to whomever he picked. And she knew then and there, with certainty, that she wanted to be around to watch him grow. Carmen too.

"What was different about your dad's grilled cheese?" she asked. "What made it better?"

"Well, my dad always used Havarti instead of cheddar. I like it better. Plus something else, but I don't know what it was."

Tears formed behind her eyes, but she promised herself she wouldn't let them fall, not in front of this sweet kid who'd lost his parents and had already witnessed so much sadness in the adults around him. She made a mental note to ask Alex if she could have copies of some photos of Carmen and Eddie's mom and dad to keep around her cabin, if he thought they would like that. She wanted to help them remember, and she wanted it to be clear that she and Alex had no intention of trying to take their place.

But they could still be a family.

"I think I know what it was," she said.

Eddie looked up at her, eyes wide.

"He was your dad, and he loved you. That's all it would take to make his sandwiches taste better."

After a beat, Eddie gave a firm nod. "I think you're right," he said.

They sat a few more moments in companionable silence, then Eddie spoke.

"What kind of tea is that?" he asked as she lifted it for a sip.

Gina grinned behind the mug. "Echinacea," she said.

His forehead wrinkled in concern. "Uh-oh. Are you getting a cold, Miss Gina?"

"Nope," she answered. "It just made me think of someone I like very much."

This earned her a grin.

"And it's good for the immune system," Eddie added.

Gina chuckled. "And there's that."

"What did I miss?" Alex asked, rising up from the couch, careful not to jostle his still-dozing niece. He scooped her gently off his lap and lay her down among a nest of blankets and pillows that Gina had spread across the floor. She rubbed her eyes but didn't wake, so Alex slid down the couch, closer to Gina and Eddie's chair.

"We're just having a chat," Eddie said.

"Can I join you?"

"Of course," Gina said. The three of them talked for another hour about everything and nothing.

Gina told them about making new cushions for Estelle's old set of dining room chairs. Eddie chatted about his favorite classes at school and which teachers he liked the best, and Alex, to Gina's surprise, shared that in the near future, he hoped to meet with a friend to find out how to convert the ranch into an organic farm.

"It's a huge undertaking," he said, determination in his voice. "But I'd really like to move the family's business in a direction that's better for the planet."

"I love that," Gina said.

He tilted his head and his lips turned up. "Do you?"

She nodded and his eyes latched on to hers. "Maybe we can work on that together," he suggested.

"As a family," Eddie said.

"As a family," Alex echoed.

"I'd like that," she said, her throat tightening with emotion as she smiled at her two favorite guys. "I'd like that very much.

Chapter Thirteen

Alex woke the next morning with a warm barnacle stuck to his side. Turning to discover it was Eddie, still conked out, he peeled the kid off as gently as he could and made his way to Gina's kitchen for a glass of water.

Morning light was just peeking over the horizon as he downed the water and started to search for coffee. Not wanting to wake Gina or the kids just yet, he brewed enough for two and set the pot to warm, then found fresh cream in the fridge. Peeking at the shelves, he saw telltale signs of his mom. There was no way Gina would have bought that much food. He chuckled, making a mental note to ask later if she wanted him to take some off her hands.

His mom was wonderful, but he'd have to talk to her about this. The way things were going between him and Gina, he didn't want to run the risk of Rosa Trevino scaring her off by continually loading her down with enough grub to feed a small army.

Speaking of a small army, something tugged at him.

Carrying his steaming coffee, he took a turn around the living room where he and the kids had spent the night, after much opposition from Gina who had insisted they were guests and should therefore take the bed.

Lifting the blanket from Eddie who was still snoozing, Alex's gut twisted.

Where was Carmen?

"Carmen," he called out, ignoring Eddie's groan of protest at the noise. "Carmen!"

A sound came from the bedroom, and Gina pulled open the door she'd left cracked during the night. "Is something wrong?" she asked, eyes bleary.

Alex raced into the bedroom, touching her shoulder as he passed. "Is Carmen in here?"

Please let her be in here, he prayed to anyone who might listen.

His heart thundered against his rib cage as he tugged back the bedsheets.

"Oh my God," he said. "Where is Carmen?"

"What?" Gina said, her voice taking on the worry in his own.

The color drained from her face, and her eyes darted around the room.

"Check the bathroom," she said, following Alex as he hurried out into the main area toward the one bath.

As fear threaded up his spine, sending a chill through his entire body, Alex yanked open the door, searching the small space within seconds.

"She's not in here," he said, meeting Gina's terrified eyes.

"What's going on?" Eddie asked, rubbing his face as he came toward him and Gina.

Alex rested a hand on his shoulder, willing his own emotions to calm so that he wouldn't scare his nephew.

Was there something to be scared of, or was his niece simply hiding somewhere?

He wouldn't allow himself to consider the former as he rushed around the small cabin with Gina right behind him, opening cabinets and checking behind every door, under every piece of furniture.

When they'd all but ransacked the place, calling his niece's name, Alex was at a loss.

"It's all my fault," Gina cried out. "It's my fault she's missing!"

"What do you mean?" Alex asked, closing the space between them.

He reached for her, but she pulled away and wouldn't let him hold her.

She pressed her fingers to her eyes, then ran her hands into her hair, grabbing the wild curls and tugging at them in distress.

"When we got in last night, I forgot to lock the door," she said, her voice loud and laced with urgency. "I should have checked before we went to bed, but I didn't think about it and—"

"Hey," he said firmly. "This is not your fault. I'm their uncle…their parent. Even though we spent the night at your house, they're under my care and they are my responsibility."

She shook her head quickly, her red-rimmed eyes full of agony.

"No, no, no," she said, tearing at her locks again. "I want to be responsible for them, too. I should never have been so careless."

His heart jolted as he realized what she was saying, but there wasn't time to think about that now.

"Come on," he said, looking between Gina and a frightened Eddie. "Let's go find her. Together."

If something happened to that girl, Gina would never forgive herself.

Why, oh why hadn't she checked the door last night?

Even as focused as she was on searching, she couldn't stop the frantic thoughts. When had she opened the door and walked out? What if she'd gotten lost somewhere on the ranch, or, God forbid, on the road! There were animals on the ranch, some of them dangerous when agitated and others, wild ones like coyotes and even the occasional bobcat, well, they could be worse. What if someone had seen her and picked her up? What if…

"You can't do that to yourself," Alex said, reading her thoughts.

He reached for her hand as they traipsed down the trail from the cabin into a wooded area. He and Eddie took turns calling Carmen's name. After her voice cracked a few times, Gina had decided to stay quiet, afraid of making things worse for the two of them.

"I can't help it," she murmured. Tears were so close, but she couldn't cry. Not when Alex must be just as worried as she. It would only make things worse.

"This isn't your fault, Gina. Let go of that idea and let's focus on finding her. She can't have gone far and the weather's nice."

Less than a mile away, the creek flowed, its normally soothing sound sending shivers up Gina's spine. *Oh God.* Her heart sank as another terrible thought crept into her overwhelmed brain. *The creek!*

That gentle sound, one of her favorite things about living in the cabin and opening her windows at night, was suddenly the most menacing thing she'd ever heard.

"Alex, what if she went down to the creek?"

He pulled in a breath. "That's where we're headed."

Gina bit her lip to keep from whimpering.

"Carmen knows how to swim," Eddie said softly, resting a hand on Gina's arm. "She'll be okay."

"He's right," Alex said.

Silently, Gina nodded. They knew Carmen best, and despite her small size and age, she was a smart cookie. Maybe everything would be okay.

It *had* to be okay. Her family had to be okay.

But her chest continued to tighten, and her insides knotted with fear and dread.

Alex stopped dead in his tracks, and Eddie and Gina swerved to keep from bumping into him.

"Did you hear that?" he asked, arms out, palms down.

Something rustled in the weeds nearby.

"Carmen!" Gina screamed at the top of her lungs. She wouldn't rest until they found her. "Carmen!"

"Miss Gina!" came a cry. "Uncle Alex?"

"Carmen!" Alex shouted, taking off in the direction of her voice.

Eddie and Gina raced after him. In the distance, she spotted the little girl's purple pajamas, the best thing she'd ever laid eyes on.

Rushing toward her, Alex scooped her into his arms. As he did, a bundle fell from her hands.

"Don't ever run off like that again," Alex said, his high-pitched voice alarming his niece.

"I'm sorry, Uncle Alex," she said on the verge of tears.

"What were you thinking?" he asked, as Eddie and Gina came in closer.

Gina reached up to brush tangled hair out of Carmen's eyes, and the little girl's lip trembled as she pointed at the ground beneath them.

"I just wanted to pick some flowers for Miss

Gina," she said, the tears coming as she buried her face in Alex's undershirt.

"Oh, honey," Alex said, meeting Gina's eyes. The fear had gone from his, replaced by obvious relief.

Gina wished she could feel the same, but as she watched the little family holding on to one another, the belonging she'd felt the day and night before, the sense that she was becoming a part of them, dissolved.

"Let's go home," Alex said, putting Carmen up on his shoulders. Holding his niece with one hand, he reached out the other for Gina to take.

She stared at it, heart still racing with the horror of what her carelessness might have caused had Carmen wandered any farther from the cabin.

"Gina?" Alex urged.

She nodded, but she didn't take his hand. Hurt marking his features, he finally let it drop, and they walked back toward the cabin, a place which no longer felt like home.

Back at the cabin after Alex had taken the kids home to the ranch house, Gina packed, grabbing the things that were hers and leaving the ones she'd been given.

She knew what she had to do, and she couldn't

take anything that would remind her of the Trevino family's kindness.

Packing the bags she'd arrived with only a short time ago, she loaded her car, locked the cabin door as she should have done the night before and tucked the key above the doorframe, then started down the road back to her sister's.

As gravel turned into pavement, she wouldn't let herself look in the rearview mirror, knowing she didn't deserve another glimpse at what might have been her only chance to finally come home.

"You can't leave," Sophie pleaded. "You have to go back there and talk to him. This wasn't your fault."

Gina cut her sister a look.

"Whose fault was it then?" she said, raising her voice. "I'm the one who let them stay over and left the door unlocked with kids around." Folding her arms across her chest, she shook her head. "I'm not fit to be around kids. It runs in the family."

"Oh, sweetheart," Sophie said, coming to sit next to her on the sofa. "You can't really believe that."

"Of course I do," Gina said, raising her palms. "Look at where we came from. Our own mom and dad didn't want us!"

Sophie rested a hand on Gina's knee, then spoke firmly. "So are you saying I shouldn't be a mom someday if I want to? Because if you're not fit to be a parent, then neither am I. We came from the same place, you know. It only follows that—"

Gina looked down at her empty hands. "Mom didn't leave until after I was born. And then Dad went downhill after." Looking up, she met her sister's eyes. "It was me who caused things to fall apart, not you."

Sophie wrapped her arms around Gina's shoulders and the two held each other.

"You know that's absolute crap, don't you?" Sophie finally said, wiping away Gina's tears. "It's not your fault Carmen got out of the house. It could, and does, happen to a lot of parents. Kids are escape artists. I see it all the time at story hour."

"Yeah, but I wanted to be better. I wanted to prove to myself that I wasn't cut from the same cloth as Mom and Dad, that I could be a good parent if the chance came. It did, and I screwed it up completely. Alex will never be able to trust me after this, and why should he? Those kids are the most important thing in his world, and I couldn't even keep them safe."

Sophie placed a hand on Gina's back and kept

it there while her sister lowered her head into her hands, crying softly.

"What is it you're *really* afraid of?" she asked.

Gina looked up, swiping at her eyes with the back of her hand. "What do you mean?"

Sophie blinked. "I mean, you've always said you're a little intimidated by the thought of kids, and you worry you'll follow in Mom and Dad's irresponsible footsteps. But you love Carmen and Eddie. I can see it clear as the nose on your face."

She reached out and booped Gina's nose with a fingertip.

"And they love you, and Alex does too."

Gina opened her mouth to protest, but Sophie held up a finger to stop her. "Don't argue with me. I'm your older sister. I know stuff."

Staying silent for several seconds, Gina thought about the question. Thoughts swirled in her mind. As much as she wanted to deny it, she knew Sophie was right. She had felt that the kids wanted her around, and maybe it did go so far as love. And Alex had all but said the word a few times, though she knew he was hesitant because of their past. He was letting her set the pace this time, afraid to freak her out.

"I guess I don't know what I'm really afraid of."

"Might I hazard a guess?" Sophie asked. "On

account of I know you pretty damn well and can see what's going on here, and I can't let you mess up the best thing that's ever happened to you."

Gina rolled her eyes and stifled a grin. "I know you're going to anyway, whether I want you to or not, so fine, go ahead."

Sophie leveled her with a stern look.

"I don't think you're afraid of raising kids, or of loving Alex. I think what you're really afraid of is getting everything you've always wanted but haven't had the courage to reach for—a family, a home. With him. You're afraid of settling down in Peach Leaf and becoming just like Mom and Dad, disillusioned with small-town life and the things that people can say and do to hurt us."

Gina looked out Sophie's apartment window at the street below. It was still the town she'd grown up in, but things had changed. People had changed. And maybe Gina just hadn't been able to accept either enough to move on.

"You're nothing like our parents. Mom was a mess, and I know that better than you because I was around for longer, and Dad was lost and in pain with *and* without her. He didn't do right by us, Gina."

She reached out and brushed hair out of Gina's eyes.

"But you have Alex, and those kids adore you. They wouldn't ask you to spend time around them if you were anything like Mom and Dad, and you know it."

Weeping now, she let her sister's words wash over her, knowing there was truth in them. Then she grabbed Sophie and pulled her in for a big hug.

"Now," Sophie said after a few moments, "pull yourself together. You've got a family to see."

Chapter Fourteen

Alex pounded on the bookstore door, calling out in desperation. "Sophie! Are you there?"

In his rush to reach her after finding the note in Gina's cabin, Alex had left his phone behind.

"Hello!"

Surely she'd be there with her sister.

For the second time that day, he'd lost someone he loved, and for the second time, he wouldn't stop looking until he found her.

"Gina!"

"Hey, hey, everything's okay," Sophie said, her head peeking out from the apartment window above the store. She studied him, taking in his disheveled appearance. "Come on up the back."

She pointed to the alley that led to the rear of the store and he nodded, running in that direction and bounding up the steps to her door.

When he got there, it opened and Sophie motioned for him to come in. He found Gina on the couch, her eyes swollen and wet with tears. He strode toward her, wanting so badly to reach for her, to pull her close and stroke her hair. But her note had been clear. She didn't feel like she was worthy of being part of his family. He knew her better than that. He knew that what she was, was scared. And he'd come to convince her to stay anyway.

"There you are," he said, stuffing his hands into his pockets as he sat next to her. "I thought I'd lost you again."

Relief flooded through him. Relief that she hadn't gone far. Relief that her eyes were filled with the love he was certain he'd been feeling from her. And relief that he still had a chance.

At least he hoped he did.

She looked up at him, her eyes full of pain. But there was something else there, too. Something that looked like the same hope he was clinging to.

"I'm still here," she said.

His throat tightened. "I'm glad," he said simply, knowing if he said more, he'd break down too.

He looked at Sophie, who gave him a smile and a nod, then stepped out of the room to give them space.

"Gina, what happened was unfortunate, but everything turned out okay." Tentatively, he took her hands in his. "It was an accident. If Jesse and I had known—I mean…if I'd known the kids would be spending time with you there, with us there, I would have child-proofed the place. Put all those little cabinet-closer things on and all the special locks, all that stuff. But when you said you needed a place, I jumped at the chance to have you back, even if it meant you just lived nearby."

Her eyes searched his.

"I didn't let myself hope that you would want us, all of us, in your life. I wanted that, more than anything, but I didn't expect it."

She squeezed his hand.

"I'm still learning all this parent stuff too," he said. "I'm not great at it yet. I miss things, but I'll get there. And you will too, if you stay."

"Oh, Alex, I'm so sorry."

She folded herself into his arms and he held her there for several moments, running his hands over her soft golden curls, feeling her heartbeat against his.

"I do want to stay," she said, wiping her eyes.

"I want to build my business, and if you'll have me, I want to build a life with you and the kids."

"Are you sure?" he asked. "I know you wanted more than that back then. You wanted to see the world. I've come to accept that, Gina, and if you go again, I'll follow this time, kids and all. I'll give up the ranch and move away from everything I know here. For you. I should have done that before, and I'm more sorry than I can say, that I didn't."

She closed her eyes, shaking her head. "Alex, no. Your home is here, and I'm happy about that. Especially because I know now that it's my home too. And I want to be here, with you, and with Carmen and Eddie."

His heart filled with the hopes and dreams he'd denied himself for years, especially after losing his father and his brother and sister-in-law. He'd done what he knew was best and taken the kids as his own, thinking that would be enough to keep him happy for years to come. But he'd been kidding himself. He could never be happy without the woman he loved. Had always loved.

"I've been all over the place already, Alex," she continued. "I've seen the world. But making a home with you, being a family, is its own kind of adventure."

He pulled her closer, kissing her with all the

pent-up feelings that had built since she'd been gone. And she kissed him back, wrapping her arms tight around him.

When they separated, she gave him a hesitant look. "So, can I move back into the cabin?"

Her face fell when he shook his head no.

"Oh, okay," she said. "Yeah, that's probably for the best. I can probably stay here with Soph until I find a—"

He pressed a finger against her lips.

"Of course you can move back if you want," he explained. "But I was really hoping you might want to move into the main house with me. We can make your cabin into a studio for your business."

Gina's hands flew to her mouth as more tears began to fall.

But this time, Alex hoped, the happy kind.

* * * * *

Try these other heartfelt romances about
second chances and fresh starts:

The Trouble with Exes
By Sera Taino

The Marine's Second Chance
By Victoria Pade

All's Fair in Love and Wine
By Michele Dunaway

Available now wherever
Harlequin Special Edition
books are sold!

Chapter One

Rafe Reyes woke when something very wet and cold touched his nose. His wake-up call was usually his daughter Susan's little finger jabbing him awake.

He blinked and rubbed his eyes, and a big ball of golden fur tried to French-kiss him.

"Bleh!" Rafe sat up, rubbing saliva off his mouth.

"Oh, he's so *cute*." Susan giggled. "Sub loves you. He gave you a kiss!"

"He gave me a slobber."

Susan stood by his bedside, still wearing her Little Mermaid pajamas. Her dimpled smile and bright blue eyes never failed to tug a smile out of him. He'd need to do something about her hair today. Blonde waves swirled around her face and tangled at her shoulders. Pigtails today? Maybe braids. He'd become an expert at both.

She bent to hug Yellow Submarine, a Labrador retriever and her new best friend. From the moment she'd met him yesterday, they'd been inseparable. Sub, for short, had appointed himself Susan's shadow.

"I want to go to the beach. I want to take Sub! He can chase me, and we can build castles."

The cobwebs in Rafe's brain slowly began to unfurl. Oh, yeah, he'd promised her the beach today.

"Okay, baby. Give Daddy a minute to put a shirt on."

He and Susan were staying in the converted lighthouse belonging to Cole Kinsella, who had been a navy SEAL and served in the same team as Rafe's best friend, Max Del Toro. Cole and his wife, Valerie, had been kind enough to put him and Susan up. Coming to Charming for Max's wedding week meant Rafe had pulled Susan out of preschool for a couple of weeks, causing yet another argument with Liz. But it was summer, and the first time he'd had a visitation with Susan for this long since the divorce. He didn't see any harm in their daughter enjoying a stay in the small, bucolic Texas Gulf Coast town.

This was the first vacation he'd had in years, and a welcome break from life in the big city of Dallas. He detested city living but Liz had a good job with a defense contractor firm. They'd moved to Texas from Atlanta, where she'd formerly been stationed, in one last attempt to save their crumbling marriage.

Rafe pulled a T-shirt over his head. "Last one to the kitchen is a rotten egg!"

Because every day he tried to be the father Susan deserved, Rafe gave her a head start. Sub didn't need one as he bounded down the steps ahead of them both. Susan skipped down the winding staircase that had been repurposed from an old ship, holding on to the rail.

Rafe was still in a state of amazement caused by the converted lighthouse. Upstairs on the outdoor deck, an old-fashioned telescope made it possible to get a spectacular view of the gulf. There were portholes for windows, a modern kitchen and a living room with one of Cole's old surfboards serving as a coffee table. Wood floors gleamed. Nautical themes were everywhere, but one might expect this from the home of a surfing enthusiast and former SEAL.

On the landing, Rafe swept Susan up in his arms. "Somebody didn't get her morning tickle!"

Susan dissolved in a flurry of squeals and laughter, trying her best to get away from the tickle monster. The kitchen was still quiet; no sign of Cole or Valerie awake.

He set Susan's wiggling body down. "What do you want for breakfast?"

"Pancakes!" Susan twirled around the kitchen. "With chocolate chips!"

Rafe had been told to make himself at home. During his stay he planned to be indispensable to the couple expecting their first child. They had saved him hundreds of dollars on a hotel room. His merely adequate salary as a Dallas firefighter didn't allow much for extras like vacations in coastal beach towns.

Making his hosts breakfast seemed like a good place to start paying back the favor.

"Good idea. Even Cole and Valerie will appreciate my chocolate chip pancakes." He got busy looking through cabinets for a pan, flour and ingredients. "Do you want to help?"

"Of course, I'm a great helper."

Zero lack of confidence in this one. Then again, she parroted nearly everything he said. He'd learned early on that kids came with no subterfuge or filter.

For this reason, and many others, he watched what he said in her presence.

"You *are* a great helper." Rafe cracked an egg into the bowl and handed her a spoon to stir.

"When I was a little girl, I didn't know how to do this but now I'm old, so I know."

He smirked. "Yes, Susan. You're old now."

She meant *older,* of course, but her four-year-old conversational skills were still developing when it came to time. It wasn't quite linear to her.

"Mommy's old. And *you're* old."

Rafe might only be thirty-three, but he sometimes felt ten years older. Susan had utterly domesticated him, which he figured had everything to do with it. He was the weekend dad who filled his days with his daughter, taking her to parks and museums. Other than his work for the Dallas Fire Department, and Susan, he had no life. He didn't date. Sadly, he'd become boring. But he hadn't planned on being a divorced single dad at his age. He'd had no plans to marry, either. And when he'd pictured marriage, someday, it was only to the woman he'd loved for half his life.

But you blew that possibility to smithereens.

Yeah, best not to think about Jordan Del Toro. He'd see her soon enough, which would be as pleasant as a root canal without anesthesia and hurt twice as much.

Susan was still working on her first pancake, light eater that she was, while Rafe had already consumed three. Valerie and Cole came down the staircase a few minutes later, visible from the kitchen due to the open floor plan and vaulted ceilings.

"Good morning, you two," Valerie said, mussing Susan's hair.

Cole fist-bumped with Rafe. "You didn't have to do all this."

"My pleasure. As my daughter will tell you, I'm the pancake whisperer."

"*Chocolate chip* pancakes?" Valerie said. "Ever since I got pregnant, I've been craving chocolate. I think I love you."

"No, you don't." Cole hooked an arm around his bride. "You love *me*."

"I was talking to the pancake, but I would love you even more if you'd cook me anything with chocolate." She gave him a quick kiss.

Rafe would have given his left heart ventricle to have had this kind of a marriage. But contrary to some cultural and religious beliefs, love didn't necessarily grow because two people were committed to each other. It didn't take root and flourish because those two people were compatible and desperately wanted to make their family work. Rafe had learned the hard way that you couldn't help whom you loved. He and Liz had done their best to give Susan the home she deserved but in the end they'd failed miserably. He'd managed to be a good father, but he'd done a poor job as Liz's husband.

"What are your plans today?" Rafe asked, handing them both a plate of pancakes. "I promised Susan the beach."

"Can we please take Sub with us?" Susan piped in. "He really loves me."

"Sure can. Sub loves the beach." Cole said. "I'll go with you guys. I haven't surfed for a week."

"I'm going to the dress fitting," Valerie said, covering her pancake with syrup. "This is going to be a disaster. Ava has us wearing strapless dresses."

"What's wrong with that?" Rafe asked.

"Well, I'm a lot bigger than normal. *Everywhere*."

"Don't worry, Jordan has this all under control," Cole said. "If she has to sew brand-new dresses for y'all I have no doubt she would do it."

"Tell her I said hello," Rafe said, knowing Jordan would be a lot more receptive to a secondhand greeting through Valerie.

"Why don't you take Valerie?" Cole suggested. "That way you can say hello yourself."

Ah, Cole was taking pity on Rafe. Kind of him. "Thanks, but I told Susan we'd hit the beach."

"I can do that," Cole said.

"No surfing." Valerie pointed. "Taking care of Susan will be good practice for you."

"We'll chase waves and build sandcastles," Cole said.

"Is that okay with you?" Rafe tipped his daughter's chin up to meet his gaze.

"I'm not a baby anymore. Sub will take care of me."

Cole splayed his hands. "Hey, what about me? Why do I always lose to Sub?"

"*Cole* will take care of you," Rafe corrected. "He's in charge. When he tells you to do something, you'll do it. Are we clear?"

Susan bobbed her head up and down. "Yeah, bro. I got it."

Cole burst into laughter and fist-bumped Susan. "Genius."

"I'll go take a shower and get ready," Rafe said.

At least he'd see Jordan Del Toro for the first time in a public setting where if she wanted to draw and quarter him, she'd be forced to reconsider.

Still, he hadn't been this nervous since the day he'd come home to tell Jordan he'd be marrying someone else.

Jordan Del Toro handled chaos, and weddings were her specialty. Weddings were 80 percent of her event planning business, Jordan Makes Plans, and she'd seen some…stuff. There was this one time when guests had thought it cute to blow bubbles toward the bride and groom as they entered the reception hall. But it had rained the night before, making the wood deck slick enough for a bride wearing three-inch heels to nearly slip and fall. Thankfully, the groom had moved fast enough to hold up the bride. Crisis averted.

Then there was the bridesmaid Jordan had found outside the reception venue, passed out drunk, her left boob hanging out of the *strapless* dress. Jordan had helped provide coverage while the girl shoved the boob back into place, then led the bridesmaid to the ladies' room so she could splash water on her face. She'd pumped her full of coffee. Crisis averted.

Yet another time, the groom was found making out with the maid of honor. Crisis *not* averted. She couldn't win them all.

But for the wedding of her older brother, Max,

to Ava Long, every crisis would be averted. She had experience. She had chutzpah. She had skills.

She had two senior citizens insisting that there be a poetry reading in place of a first dance.

"I've written a poem for Max and Ava that they will adore," Patsy Villanueva said. "It's quite romantic, if I do say so myself, and I've censored some of the spicier details since children will be present."

"Instead of erotic poetry, I suggest quoting from the classics. Perhaps Shakespeare. Or Emily Dickinson. She was a true romantic." This was from Etta May Virgil, president of the local senior citizen poetry group named the Almost Dead Poet Society.

Yes, they had a president.

"Emily Dickinson?" Patsy shook her head. "Poor woman. I suggest Jane Austen. Perhaps something from *Emma*? Or *Pride and Prejudice*?"

"Jane Austen was not a *poet*," Etta May said.

"I bet to differ," said Patsy.

Jordan took a sip of the strong brew supplied by Ava's coffee company and served by the Salty Dog Bar & Grill. Her brother and two of his best friends owned and ran the place where she now sat and tried to relax before her appointments today.

"All sound like wonderful ideas," Jordan lied. "I'll run them by Ava just as soon as I can."

"See?" Mrs. Villanueva elbowed Etta May. "I knew she'd listen."

Waving, they both went back to their booth.

Jordan had arrived late last night to Charming, Texas, from her home in Santa Cruz, California, two weeks before the wedding. Because for the first time in her career, she'd planned a wedding *long-distance*. Also for the first time, she was a bridesmaid *and* wedding planner. The rest of the Del Toro clan would arrive next week, but she was far too much of a control freak not to be present ahead of time. Everything would go according to her carefully laid plans. She'd arrived early enough to anticipate, and avert, any crisis. This was her brother's wedding, after all, and *nothing* could go wrong. It had to be perfect.

She told herself it was her constant desire to achieve utter perfection that was making her anxious, and not the thought of seeing Rafe for the first time in four years.

Jordan consulted the leather planner that rarely left her presence. Old-school, sure, but it worked for her. She was a tactile and visual person to the nth degree. To that end, she'd planned nearly every minute of the fourteen days she'd be in Charming. Final cake testing, dress fitting, picking up wedding favors, caterer details, videographer and flowers. A trip to the beach had been scheduled in or her sister Maribel would accuse her of being a workaholic. By her calculations, this left zero minutes to reconnect, or otherwise chat, with Rafe. There would be no small talk or "happy" reunion.

She would say a quick hello to both his daughter and wife, Liz, and Rafe, too, since it could not be avoided, and stay busy every second until Geoff Costner arrived. Geoff, her attorney boyfriend extraordinaire of two years, happened to be the best plus-one a woman could ever hope for. He was handsome, a great flirt, knew how to dance, and was going to make Rafe rue the day.

Both her present and future looked bright, and soon enough she'd marry Geoff. They were perfect for each other, as all his colleagues continually reminded them. A month ago, he'd suggested they get married rather than continue to live in separate condos. He was right, of course, and even if it wasn't the most romantic proposal, it certainly was the most practical.

Since he hadn't officially asked, she'd simply told him sure, it was a good idea. Then she'd waited for a ring, or something a little more… romantic. When it didn't come, she realized that

Geoff just wasn't the type. It would be up to her as the organizer half of the couple to firm up details and choose a date. He was a good man. Sure, he lacked skills in the romance department, but she could do without those. Romantic and passionate men tended to be over the top and, more often than not, their fervor burned itself out. Been there, done that. She was a lot smarter now.

"Sorry we're late." Ava bustled up to the booth, two older women in tow. She took a seat across from Jordan. "Jordan, this is my mother, Dr. Katherine Long, and Lucia Perez, the woman who helped raise me."

Dr. Long resembled her daughter, but contrary to the always colorful Ava, was dressed in a classy black monochrome pantsuit. The matronly woman, Ava's former nanny and practically a member of the family, had beautiful latte skin and short salt-and-pepper hair. She wore a bright, multicolored skirt and matching top. From the beginning, Jordan had asked enough questions of Ava to know that they were basically dealing with not one mother of the bride, but *two*.

"Are you both attending the cake testing?" Jordan consulted her planner. This was the first appointment today, but she didn't have a note in that regard.

"Is that a problem?" Dr. Long exchanged a look with Lucia. "We had both planned for this."

"Of course not," Jordan said, snapping her book shut. "The more the merrier."

"*Ay, muy bueno,* I came all the way from Colombia," Lucia said in her thick accent. "What a special time this is."

"They both just want to be a part of our day," Ava said, her usual bubbly self.

Jordan had first met her future sister-in-law when she visited the Del Toro family in Watsonville, California, last Christmas. There was no way anyone could meet the effervescent Ava Long and not instantly like her. The only surprise was that someone as grumpy and uptight as her former navy SEAL brother had wound up with a Miss Sunshine.

"Would anyone like some coffee first or should we get going?" Jordan glanced at her Fitbit watch.

Efficient, because it gave her the time, how many steps she'd taken in a day, and her heart rate. That last one was important because Jordan fully expected it to blow into the triple digits and for the first time not due to a difficult bride.

"We had coffee at the hotel," Dr. Long explained. "And I skipped breakfast so that I could eat as many samples as possible."

"I'm ready when you are," Ava said. "First, cake testing. Next, dress fittings."

Jordan climbed out of the booth. "We should get going. I like to be early."

Early or on time were the only timelines on Jordan's radar. She'd said goodbye to her carefree ways long ago.

Chapter Two

Not every wedding planner attended bridal fittings, but not only was this a family affair, Jordan also overstressed about strapless dresses after the bridesmaid's boobage fiasco. And Ava had chosen a royal blue strapless bridesmaid dress, though she had one bridesmaid who was six months pregnant. To say Jordan was *concerned* would be putting it mildly. It definitely wasn't the most practical idea. If asked, she'd have given her expert opinion. No. Just. No.

After the cake testing, Jordan had arrived early to the only wedding boutique in town and now sat alone, consulting her planner. A typical wedding shop, Charmed, I'm Sure was filled with racks of white gowns and a small pedestal in the center of the room surrounded by three-way mirrors. As part of her due diligence, Jordan had alerted the stylist of her concerns with the strapless dress.

All things considered, the cake testing had gone smoothly earlier. The two "mothers" affectionately slugged it out between four-tiers and six-tiers. Dr. Long thought four-tiers were sufficient. But Lucia insisted there be at least six, because everybody should be allowed to indulge on this special day. Finally, to end the standoff, Jordan had reminded both women that this was Ava's day and her decision.

Not surprisingly, Ava had split the difference and gone with five tiers because she hated the thought of anyone going without.

This wedding would *not* be a small and intimate affair. A local business owner, Ava Long was the daughter of two prominent Dallas-based physicians. Max, for his part, was a former navy SEAL and a leader in their business community. Ava had campaigned to have the wedding in Charming, and as her compromise, agreed her engagement could be announced in all the major high-society venues. She had also agreed to be married in the large banquet hall of The Lookout, the only hotel in Charming, when she would have preferred City Hall and a simple reception at the Salty Dog.

Jordan was grateful for the banquet hall choice and had registered for a hotel room there. Last night, after once more checking the size of the hall and double-checking their booking time, she'd settled into her own room at The Lookout.

Briefly, she'd checked in with Geoff. "Please tell me you've already purchased your plane ticket."

"All taken care of. I had my secretary book it."

"Thank you, honey. This wedding is particularly important to me."

Geoff knew all about Rafe. But he also understood that Rafe was married, with a child, so there was zero jealousy on his part. Jordan wished there was a little pinch. It might feel nice to be wanted and reminded she was special. Geoff often got so caught up in work he'd forget the little things. He'd been involved in pretrial preparation of a civil litigation lawsuit for months and they'd both been neglecting their relationship. It would be good to get away just the two of them.

Then again, she'd been the one to avoid making plans for their wedding like setting an actual date. She was waiting, she had to admit, for a more formal ask from Geoff. But when Max announced his engagement to Ava, Jordan was reminded that she'd crossed an invisible timeline. It was time to get busy and create the happy balance of work and home life.

Ava waltzed into the boutique, pulling Jordan out of her thoughts. Max was with her.

Jordan stood, crossed her arms and jutted out her hip. "Get *out* of here. It's bad luck for the groom to see the dress."

"Stupid superstition. I'm just dropping off my bride." He kissed Ava, not so secretly palmed her butt, and then was out the door.

"I hate being apart from him for long, and he'll be in a business meeting the rest of the day," Ava gushed. "This is great, you're all business, and that's exactly what I need right now."

Jordan folded her future sister-in-law into her arms, realizing she'd come off sounding like a shrew. Leave it to Ava to let it go.

"How are you doing with all the excitement? Is it too much?" Jordan asked.

"Oh, no! Are you kidding? I love it!"

"Some brides flip out under all the pressure and anticipation. But this is why Max hired me. I don't want *you* to worry about a single thing. Just enjoy your day. Every detail, and I mean every single detail, is in my book." She then reached for and patted her planner.

"You keep it all in there?"

"Each wedding I do has their own book. Sketches, diagrams, ideas. Details. I'm the most organized person you'll ever meet, which makes me so good at what I do."

"And I *love* that I don't have to worry about a thing."

Just then the doors swung open and a beautiful brunette waltzed in.

"Stacy!" Ava rushed to meet her friend, hugging her as if they hadn't seen each other in decades.

She introduced her to Jordan, and they spent a few minutes getting acquainted.

Stacy wrung her hands together. "I've stopped breastfeeding my daughter, but honestly? My measurements have um, changed a bit. Hopefully there's enough material to expand."

"Well…" Jordan began.

This could very well be an issue.

"Of course, it's not a problem!" Ava said.

Then again, the bride was always right.

The stylist joined them. "Ava, dear, would you come with me?"

"See you both in a minute!" Ava waved.

Jordan turned to Stacy. "If there's a problem with your dress, we have time for alterations.

That's why we're…we're…" Jordan stopped talking when the doors to the shop swung open again.

Valerie Kinsella walked through the open door held by none other than Rafe.

"Hi, there," Valerie said, walking up to them. "Hope y'all don't mind but Rafe wanted to tag along."

Jordan didn't hear any other words. It was as if her world had become a silent movie. Noise became little else but muffled sounds. People talked, their lips moving, and she heard nothing but a buzzing in her ears.

Rafe. This wasn't in her planner.

He wore jeans and a T-shirt, looking so casual that Jordan suddenly felt overdressed in her pink designer jacket dress with black piping. When he stepped in front of her, over four years faded away and she was back home in Watsonville at the fruit stand where Rafe had told her he was marrying Liz.

She'd cried, pulled on him, reminded him that she loved him. Begged him not to marry Liz. In other words, utterly *humiliated* herself in front of this man.

"Jordan?"

She snapped out of it when she found Rafe staring at her curiously, head canted, a slight smile on his lips.

"Oh, hi. Rafe. Yeah. Uh-huh…good to see you again."

He enveloped her into his warm embrace and the walls she'd erected stayed intact. She patted him three times on the back in a friendship sort of way and quickly stepped back.

"I don't know what *you're* doing here. This is all about dresses and fittings. So boring for you, I'm sure."

"Normally. But I wanted to see you."

He sounded sincere. He wanted to see the girl he'd dropped like the stock market crash? Nice of him. Did he expect her to still be wounded and heartbroken? She schooled her features because this was Max's oldest friend and the best man. She'd had every intention of getting along with him but at the moment she bristled with contempt.

"Well, now you've seen me." She picked up her book and held it to her chest to discourage any more hugging.

"You look good, *cielito lindo*."

This was his old term of endearment for her, meaning *pretty sky*, and because of those same apparently *poorly* constructed walls, her heart tugged.

"Thanks, and so do you."

Still roguishly handsome, but now there were tiny lines in the corners of his eyes, giving him a mature and worldly look. As always, his very presence upset her equilibrium and threw her back to younger, and much weaker, times in her life. But even if he'd been her first love, she'd come a long way since Rafe crushed her heart.

She threw a longing look at the bridesmaids, but Stacy and Valerie were engaged in conversation and ignoring everyone else.

And Ava had still not emerged from the dressing room.

Someone please interrupt us. Please. I'm begging you.

When no savior came, she cleared her throat. "So. How are Susan and Liz?"

"Susan is with Cole at the lighthouse. They're going to hang out at the beach. And…well, Liz and I are divorced."

She blinked, completely blindsided. *"Divorced?"*

"That's right."

Why hadn't she known about this? Why hadn't Max told her?

"I'm sorry."

"Don't be. We tried to make it work, for Susan's

sake, and that's all two people who care about each other can do."

Our daughter. Even now the words cut a slice off Jordan's heart. They'd been a little family, at least for a while. It was more than Rafe had ever given her.

"Yes, I guess that's…true."

"How about you? Are you single?"

Jordan smiled, delight rising in her like water from a geyser. "No. In fact, I'm in a serious relationship. He's coming to the wedding."

"Then I look forward to meeting him."

"Good. And I look forward to you meeting him as well."

Rafe quirked a brow. "Okay."

"It's just that Geoff is everything I've ever wanted. He's loyal, devoted, and will do anything for me." A little worried she'd made Geoff sound like a dog, she made a mental note to pull back on the praise. "He also wants to start a family right away."

"I'm happy for you."

"Thanks."

"Are you planning on a big wedding?"

"Um, well, I haven't set a date. It's imminent, though."

"If he's a smart man he won't let you get away."

She blinked, a little stunned by the compliment. In the way of conversation, she had nothing that felt safe enough to bring up, so she reached.

"So, do you have a date to the wedding?"

He nodded, tipping back on his heels. "Susan is my date."

"I've heard a lot about her."

"She's smart and funny, too. You'll love her."

"I'm sure I will."

Gosh, they were being so civil to each other. Jordan had wanted to throw a goblet of champagne in his face, but she'd done a fair job of containing her anger. Besides, she'd never ruin this moment for Ava.

Speaking of Ava, all eyes turned when she sashayed out of the dressing room and stepped on the pedestal in the most incredible wedding dress Jordan had ever laid eyes on. The satin dress had a fitted bodice that flared out past her thighs in a mermaid style silhouette. Ava had the perfect figure for it. A sweetheart collar completed the look, giving her a positively royal appearance.

"Oh, Ava!" Stacy covered her mouth.

Valerie wiped away tears. "You look like Princess Grace of Monaco. Or some other princess."

"Doesn't she?" Dr. Long went behind Ava, inspecting the short and elegant flared train.

"Que bonita!" said Lucia as she joined Dr. Long.

"Your brother is one lucky guy," Rafe remarked.

"If you'll excuse me, I have to get to work."

And with that, Jordan turned away from Rafe and went back to her happy place.

Don't miss
A Charming Single Dad *by Heatherly Bell,*
available May 2023 wherever
Harlequin® Special Edition books
and ebooks are sold.

www.Harlequin.com

COMING NEXT MONTH FROM

HARLEQUIN®

SPECIAL EDITION

#2983 FORTUNE'S RUNAWAY BRIDE
The Fortunes of Texas: Hitting the Jackpot • by Allison Leigh
Isabel Banninger's fiancé is a two-timing jerk! Running out of her own wedding leads her straight into CEO Reeve Fortune's strong, very capable arms. Reeve is *so* not her type. But is he the perfect man to get this runaway bride to say "I do"?

#2984 SKYSCRAPERS TO GREENER PASTURES
Gallant Lake Stories • by Jo McNally
Web designer Olivia Carson hides her physical and emotional scars behind her isolated country life. Until a simple farmhouse remodel brings city-boy contractor Tony Vello crashing into her quiet world. They share similar past pain...and undeniable attraction. But will he stay once the job is done?

#2985 LOVE'S SECRET INGREDIENT
Love in the Valley • by Michele Dunaway
Nick Reilly adores Zoe Smith's famous chocolate chip cookies—and Zoe herself. He hides his billionaire status to get closer to the single mom. Even pretends to be her fiancé. But trading one fake identity for another is a recipe for disaster. Unless it saves Zoe's bakery *and* her guarded heart...

#2986 THE SOLDIER'S REFUGE
The Tuttle Sisters of Coho Cove • by Sabrina York
Football star Jax Stringfellow was the bane of Natalie Tuttle's high school existence. A traumatic military tour transformed her former crush from an arrogant, mean-spirited jock into a father figure for her nephews. But can the jaded TV producer trust her newfound connection with this kinder, gentler, *sexier* Jax?

#2987 THEIR ALL-STAR SUMMER
Sisters of Christmas Bay • by Kaylie Newell
Marley Carmichael is back in Christmas Bay, ready to make her baseball-announcing dreams come true. When a one-night stand with sexy minor-league star Owen Taylor ends with a surprise pregnancy, life *and* love throw her the biggest curveball yet!

#2988 A TASTE OF HOME
Sisterhood of Chocolate & Wine • by Anna James
Layla Williams is a spoiled princess—or so Wall Streeter turned EMT Shane Kavanaugh thought. But the captivating chef is so much more than he remembers. When her celebrated French restaurant is threatened by a hostile investor, he'll use all his business—and romance—skills to be the hometown hero Layla needs!

YOU CAN FIND MORE INFORMATION ON UPCOMING HARLEQUIN TITLES, FREE EXCERPTS AND MORE AT HARLEQUIN.COM.

HSECNM0423

Get 4 FREE REWARDS!

We'll send you 2 FREE Books plus 2 FREE Mystery Gifts.

FREE Value Over **$20**

Both the **Harlequin® Special Edition** and **Harlequin® Heartwarming™** series feature compelling novels filled with stories of love and strength where the bonds of friendship, family and community unite.

YES! Please send me 2 FREE novels from the Harlequin Special Edition or Harlequin Heartwarming series and my 2 FREE gifts (gifts are worth about $10 retail). After receiving them, if I don't wish to receive any more books, I can return the shipping statement marked "cancel." If I don't cancel, I will receive 6 brand-new Harlequin Special Edition books every month and be billed just $5.49 each in the U.S. or $6.24 each in Canada, a savings of at least 12% off the cover price, or 4 brand-new Harlequin Heartwarming Larger-Print books every month and be billed just $6.24 each in the U.S. or $6.74 each in Canada, a savings of at least 19% off the cover price. It's quite a bargain! Shipping and handling is just 50¢ per book in the U.S. and $1.25 per book in Canada.* I understand that accepting the 2 free books and gifts places me under no obligation to buy anything. I can always return a shipment and cancel at any time by calling the number below. The free books and gifts are mine to keep no matter what I decide.

Choose one: ☐ **Harlequin Special Edition**   ☐ **Harlequin Heartwarming**
(235/335 HDN GRJV)   **Larger-Print**
(161/361 HDN GRJV)

Name (please print)

Address   Apt. #

City   State/Province   Zip/Postal Code

Email: Please check this box ☐ if you would like to receive newsletters and promotional emails from Harlequin Enterprises ULC and its affiliates. You can unsubscribe anytime.

Mail to the **Harlequin Reader Service:**
IN U.S.A.: P.O. Box 1341, Buffalo, NY 14240-8531
IN CANADA: P.O. Box 603, Fort Erie, Ontario L2A 5X3

Want to try 2 free books from another series? Call 1-800-873-8635 or visit www.ReaderService.com.

*Terms and prices subject to change without notice. Prices do not include sales taxes, which will be charged (if applicable) based on your state or country of residence. Canadian residents will be charged applicable taxes. Offer not valid in Quebec. This offer is limited to one order per household. Books received may not be as shown. Not valid for current subscribers to the Harlequin Special Edition or Harlequin Heartwarming series. All orders subject to approval. Credit or debit balances in a customer's account(s) may be offset by any other outstanding balance owed by or to the customer. Please allow 4 to 6 weeks for delivery. Offer available while quantities last.

Your Privacy—Your information is being collected by Harlequin Enterprises ULC, operating as Harlequin Reader Service. For a complete summary of the information we collect, how we use this information and to whom it is disclosed, please visit our privacy notice located at corporate.harlequin.com/privacy-notice. From time to time we may also exchange your personal information with reputable third parties. If you wish to opt out of this sharing of your personal information, please visit readerservice.com/consumerschoice or call 1-800-873-8635. **Notice to California Residents**—Under California law, you have specific rights to control and access your data. For more information on these rights and how to exercise them, visit corporate.harlequin.com/california-privacy.

HSEHW22R3

HARLEQUIN
PLUS

Try the best multimedia subscription service for romance readers like you!

Read, Watch and Play.

Experience the easiest way to get the romance content you crave.

Start your **FREE TRIAL** at
<u>www.harlequinplus.com/freetrial</u>.